ERIN LUCERO

The North Passage

A Sequel to Quest for the Phoenix

First published by BOGHA Press 2025

First edition

ISBN: 979-8-9992742-3-6

Editing by Carrie Bolin

This book was professionally typeset on Reedsy.
Find out more at reedsy.com

The Magical Adventures of Tori and Hudson
Book 1 - Quest for the Phoenix
Book 2 - The North Passage

To the Children of the World.
You are the Inspiration and the Way.

Contents

1 The Forecast Is Hot and Humid   1

2 A Different Kind of Day   11

3 Reaching Out   19

4 The Great Reset   33

5 Coming Together   41

6 The Prophecy   51

7 The North Passage   57

8 The Veil of Illusion   75

9 This is the North Pole?   89

10 Finding the Weavers   109

11 What Happened to Gravity?   123

12 All the Children Arrive   131

13 Finding Your Thread   137

14 Resetting the System   151

15 Returning Home   159

16 A New Day   171

Epilogue   179

About the Author   183

Also by Erin Lucero   185

One

The Forecast Is Hot and Humid

Tori strolled into math class with two minutes to spare. She dropped her purple bag onto the floor next to an open wooden desk by the window. She eased into the metal chair, which was already hot from the sunlight streaming in.

It was another sweltering day, the fifth in a row. The sky was the hazy, humid gray-blue of August, not the bright blue you'd see at the beginning of June. Tori's brown curly hair was pulled back into a tight ponytail, but some curls had poked out and stuck to her face in the humid heat.

"It's a good thing it's the last day of school, Julie," Tori said to the girl sitting next to her. "I couldn't take another day in this hot box!"

"You're telling me!" the girl shook her head dramatically, long blonde hair swishing on her shoulders as she turned to look at Tori. "I was absolutely MELTING in English class. I don't think the air works in that room at all."

"Man, that's awful," Tori replied, "I'm glad I had English first period." Julie turned back to talk with another classmate, and Tori looked outside.

The green grass was already starting to brown in the heat. Her mom had been going on about climate change this morning on their drive to school. A record-breaking year of hurricanes and heat waves was predicted for the summer. Tori's family lived in farm country, and the weather was all people seemed to talk about. Worries about crops failing and the money that would be lost if the weather continued in this hot and dry pattern. Though she was so excited to be getting out of school for summer break, she wasn't looking forward to all this heat! At least her air conditioning worked well at home, unlike the school's.

Thinking about the heat, she remembered her adventure last summer, her secret Quest to save the Phoenix. She had traveled all the way to Scotland! Scotland definitely wasn't a hot place! Even in the summer, she'd worn a hoodie. She wished she could go back there, instead of melting in this classroom, waiting to be bored by math problems.

She remembered her trip down the underground rivers with her gnome friends Malcolm and Seamus on the way to Scotland. They had met Gallywomps, fairies, and even a magical horse named Ahearn. And then there was the enchanted village of Billadoon where she helped the Phoenix be reborn. It was such an incredible adventure! Multiplication and fractions were not at all interesting compared to that. A small yawn escaped as she thought about the next hour of class.

She'd told her little brother Hudson about the Quest. She had even shown him the magic journal and stone that Malcolm and Seamus had given her last fall. But she hadn't told anyone else. I mean, who else could she tell? Who would believe she'd gone on an actual quest to Scotland through underground rivers that no one had heard of and saved a Phoenix? Or that she'd healed the King of the Gallywomps with Phoenix tears? And that she, Tori, was the only person who could have done it, because she had ancient magic in her blood?

No, she couldn't think of anyone besides her brother who would believe her. She almost told her best friend Madi. But as soon as she started to talk about a garden gnome that walked and talked, she could see a look in Madi's eyes. Some things were just too much for others to believe.

As she thought of Madi, she looked towards the back of the room. Madi's seat was still empty, even on the last day of school. Tori had hoped she'd be back in school by now, but she just hadn't been ready to return. Julie, the girl next to her, saw where Tori was looking and whispered, "Can you believe she's still out? What does it even mean? A mental health crisis? She should just suck it up and get over herself."

Tori was angered by Julie's statement but kept her calm. "A mental health crisis happens because people tell us to suck it up and ignore our feelings until we can't even find a way to face the day. Madi's going through a lot right now. First, she got bullied by those girls at lunch for being on the spectrum. Then her dad lost his job, and her parents are having a rough time with money. She blames herself for all of it, like any of this is her fault. She thought hurting herself was the only way out. Have some sympathy, Julie. It could happen to any of us."

Julie shot Tori a sulky look but kept quiet. Tori had learned a lot in the last year about standing up for others and being confident in her opinion. But it didn't make it any easier to see so many people she cared about struggling.

Just as she looked at her watch, surprised that class hadn't started yet, the bell rang. Two boys came careening in the door, pushing a smaller boy aside to get inside before they were late. The little boy stumbled, and they laughed cruelly.

"Can't you see you're in our way, Cedar?" the bigger one jeered. "But that's you, isn't it? Always in the way. Always trying to fit in where no one wants you. You'd be better off just disappearing," he finished with a swoosh of his hand as if wiping Cedar from the world.

Cedar slumped into a chair, eyes downcast. The teacher spoke up and

3

called everyone to attention. No comment on what had just happened, just to get out their books so they could finish up the lesson on fractions.

Tori sighed and looked out the window again. She promised herself to message Madi after school. At least Madi would know someone cared about her.

* * *

By 3:15, all the kids in Tori's class were bouncing in their seats, waiting for the school bell to ring and summer to start. At this point, the teacher had given up on teaching and was talking about the importance of staying sharp during the summer. "Don't forget to keep up on your studies!" he said, though clearly no one was listening. He finally gave up entirely and told the class they could clean out their desks and pack their bags.

At 3:30, the bell finally rang, and Tori about ran out of class. Shouting bye to her friends and promising to meet up soon, she wove her way through the parking lot and found her mom waiting for her in their blue SUV.

Her little brother Hudson was already in the car, his long blonde curly hair cascading down to his shoulders. He was wearing an ice hockey jersey and drinking a protein shake. Tori put her backpack in the back next to his hockey gear.

"Hi Mom! Hi Hudson!" she called out as she closed the hatch and got in the passenger seat of the car. Last month, she'd gotten tall enough to move from the back seat to the front. "Are we going to Hudson's practice?"

Her mom replied, "Of course we are! It's Thursday! And hockey practice never stops, even during the summer."

Tori buckled her seat belt and smiled back at her brother. Most of the time, they got along okay, though sometimes he drove her crazy. "Oh yeah, that's right. I almost forgot what day it was. I was just so excited for school to be done!"

"Was Madi back in school for the last day?" her mom asked.

"No," Tori sighed. "But I heard she's home from the hospital. She seems to be doing better. I thought I could visit her next week. She seems pretty alone."

"I think that's a great idea, Tori," her mom said, smiling kindly at her.

As they drove to Hudson's hockey practice, the radio was tuned to the news channel, going over the day's headlines.

"Bombings continued overnight in the Middle East," the journalist droned on in a monotone voice. "The civilian casualties continue to mount on both sides. The leaders of the four countries at the heart of the conflict have been called to the UN for peace talks, but so far, discussions have gone nowhere. Fears of a broader war continue to grow, and the surrounding countries have started to make preparations by instituting drafts and stockpiling weapons."

"Mom," Hudson asked with worry in his voice, "Are they saying that war could come to us, too?"

"Oh, sorry, sweetie," Mom replied, switching the radio off. "We don't need to listen to the news anymore. I was just checking the headlines before I picked you up." She paused for a moment. "I hope everything will be fine, but honestly, I don't know anymore. Kids, we seem to be leaving you with a big mess to clean up when you're grown." Letting out a long sigh, Mom switched on an upbeat song to play from her phone.

But just as the song's happy melody started to play, she slammed on her brakes, cursing loudly at a car in front of her. "What the heck, buddy! We have kids in the car! Get off your phone and pay attention!"

Tori looked back at Hudson. He had a blank stare on his face, but she knew what he was thinking. He often talked to her about his worries and anxiety. The adults tried to make them feel safe, but the kids still knew what was going on. It was all the grown-ups talked about, how much costs had gone up, how a friend was struggling to make rent, or if politics had gotten so bad there'd be a civil war.

So Hudson worried about these things, too, even though he was only nine. He worried about wars, about what would happen if they lost their parents, or if they lost their home. He worried about money, even though his dad had a great job that paid well. Mom and Dad reassured him, but he still worried.

"Hey Hudson!" Tori brought him back from his far-off look. "Who are you playing in hockey this weekend?"

"I don't know," Hudson smiled, coming back to himself. "But I sure hope we win! Mom, who are we playing again?"

"You're playing the Jets. You played them last month and tied," she said, moving swiftly along the highway now that the traffic jam had cleared. "But your whole team has been improving a lot this month. I bet you'll win this time!"

A new song came on, and Hudson's mood improved as he thought about hockey, watching the trees go by in the car.

* * *

Tori felt like Hudson's practice was taking forever, even with her ice skating for an hour on the second rink. She was anxious to get home and officially put her school bag in the closet for the summer.

After practice, they stopped to get take-out Indian food. The sun was setting by the time they finally got home. Her three dogs greeted them loudly at the door, barking and jumping excitedly. Tori barely made it in without spilling the takeout containers.

6

"Go wash your hands and let's have dinner," her mom called out as she followed Tori into the kitchen. "And then, kids, you get to turn your alarms off! Summer break!"

Hudson cheered and zoomed upstairs immediately to turn off his bedroom alarm. Tori's was on her phone, so she'd do that when she went to bed. Instead, she set the table for the four of them and put the biggest takeout container next to her dad's seat. He loved Indian food!

"Yummy!" He called to her as he walked in from the living room and gave her a big hug. "Thanks, Tori! I'm looking forward to eating all of it, plus yours, too!" He grinned at her and then asked. "Hey, do you know where your mom is?"

"She went upstairs," Tori replied.

As he walked out of the room, she could hear him call out to their mom, then saying in a quiet voice, "Gwen, I have to talk to you later, after the kids go to bed. Some more bad news." Tori felt worried. Maybe Hudson was right to worry. Things did seem to be getting pretty bad.

She tried to put her fears aside and focus on the excitement of summer break. By the end of the evening, she'd completely forgotten about the radio's talk about war and her dad's whispered discussion.

She'd texted her friend Madi, and she was doing well. She was even up for a get-together next week. After watching some TV, she went up to her room, turned her alarm off, and fell happily asleep.

* * *

Tori woke with a start. It wasn't even light out, but she had the distinct feeling someone had been shaking her awake. She looked around and didn't see anyone. Just as she was about to turn over and go back to sleep, the bed shook. Then the things on her dresser began to shake. A book fell off the bookshelf, crashing to the ground, along with a little glass figurine. She turned on her bedside lamp as the shaking stopped.

What the heck? Tori thought to herself. *Was that an earthquake?*

They never had earthquakes where she lived. They were only supposed to be in California!

Suddenly, the house rattled again, stronger this time. More things shook and fell from the dressers and shelves.

"Mom?!?!" she heard her brother cry out in the hallway. She jumped out of bed and went to her door, also wanting to find her parents.

"Mom!?!?" she echoed, running to their parents' bedroom. "What was that? Was that an earthquake?"

Their mom came rushing out, turning on the hallway light so they could see each other. "Quick, kids, let's stand in a doorway. It's the safest place." She guided them to the bathroom's doorway and held them tight. "Dad's run outside to see what's happening, but yeah, I think that was an earthquake! I mean it must have been! I don't know what else it could be? We've never had them here before."

Hudson held on to his mom's side for dear life, and Tori wrapped herself around the other side, forming a kind of Mom sandwich. There was another rumble, the largest and longest one. A lamp fell over, crashing in the bedroom, sending glass everywhere. A bookshelf toppled over in the hallway. Shampoo bottles fell off the shelf in the shower. They heard a giant tree crash to the ground outside, and the floor shook beneath them. The lights flickered off and on as the whole house trembled.

After what felt like an eternity, the shaking stopped.

The three of them stood huddled in the doorway for another few minutes, not sure if the earthquake was over. Their dad came up the stairs two at a time to check on them. "Are you okay?" Relief washed over his face when he saw the three standing there, shaken, but safe. He continued, "Everything seems to be standing. But what the heck was that? An earthquake? Here? I've never heard of such a thing!"

As they exhaled in relief that it was over, their phones started dinging with notifications.

An emergency alert text came through, screeching with a high-pitched alarm.

SHELTER IN PLACE ORDER. MULTIPLE EARTHQUAKES DETECTED. SEEK SHELTER INSIDE IN A SECURE AREA SUCH AS A DOORWAY OR UNDER A TABLE. AUTHORITIES WILL UPDATE SOON.

A news notification came up on her mom's feed.

EARTHQUAKES ERUPT ALONG THE ENTIRE EASTERN SEABOARD. MULTIPLE CASUALTIES REPORTED.

"Rob, look at this," she showed her phone to Tori's Dad. "It wasn't just here."

He read the first few lines of the article. "It must have been the entire fault line that gave way. This is insane. Let's see if we can find out anything more. We can go downstairs to the kitchen. We should be safe there."

Tori and Hudson held their mom's hands as they all went downstairs, avoiding the many fallen objects on the floor. Their dad brought out his laptop. Scanning the different news feeds, his eyes grew more furrowed by the minute. Meanwhile, their mom was scrolling through her phone while Tori and Hudson stayed by her side. "What the... No way... It can't be.. This is insane…" she exclaimed.

Tori and Hudson could both see the images on the screen, and what they saw didn't look good at all. Piles of rubble instead of buildings, fires, people on the street walking around in fear and confusion, and great cracks in the road. The more their mom scrolled through the images, the more frightened Tori became. What was going on?

"Kids," she finally said to them. "This earthquake we felt happened everywhere. I mean like, EVERYWHERE. All over the world. The whole world has just ripped open." Their dad nodded solemnly, agreeing. "Let's take a minute. Don't panic. We'll figure this thing out. We're on a farm with plenty of resources. We'll be okay, kids."

Just as he said that, another huge tremor erupted from the Earth, shaking the entire house. Dishes fell on the floor, and pictures jumped off the wall, glass shattering as they fell. The lights flickered. Then they went out. And stayed out.

They all clung to each other in the darkness, Mom and Dad protecting Tori and Hudson in a tight hug. Finally, after what felt like an hour, the shaking stopped. Their mom looked tentatively at her phone to see if another notification would come through, but nothing. Up at the right corner, it showed zero bars. No service.

The dogs came running into the kitchen, whining, frightened at all the commotion. Hudson grabbed the smallest one in a fierce hug. And then all was silent.

* * *

Two

A Different Kind of Day

For a few minutes, everyone stood in silence.

But after there seemed to be no more quakes, they cautiously separated from the tight huddle they'd formed and began to look around.

Tori's dad went outside to see about starting the generator to get the lights and power going. Her mom walked around the house assessing all the things that had fallen or broken.

Tori and Hudson stayed in the kitchen, soothing the dogs who licked their hands and faces, and trying to keep them away from the broken glass. Hudson jumped up. "Do you think the chickens are okay?"

They had a chicken coop outside surrounded by tall trees. He worried that the tree they heard fall could have landed on the coop. "Mom, I'm going to go check on the chickens!" He raced out of the house barefoot, barely avoiding broken glass and shattered plates.

Tori followed, but remembered to put her shoes on and brought the dogs outside with her.

As she stepped outside, she saw the sky starting to lighten in the

11

pre-dawn. It was still dark but bright enough to see. A few trees had fallen over in the field by the house, but none onto the chicken coop. The driveway had cracks cutting through the asphalt, and some of the hillside looked like it had slid down, forming a big pile of dirt and rubble at the bottom. She looked up to their barn at the top of the hill, and saw it was still standing. Overall, things seemed okay at the farm. But then Tori looked up above the tree line.

She could see gray smoke darkening the sky, even as the rest of the sky grew brighter. "What's that?" she called out to Hudson, pointing above the trees. They ran up the driveway as their house was at the bottom of a hill. They stopped when they could see over the trees. The gray smoke also had a red-orange hue, like it was coming from a fire. They turned around to get a full view of the sky. In five or six different places, smoke and fire wafted into the air. In the distance, they heard a fire truck siren. They ran back down the hill, dogs following behind, to tell their parents what they'd seen.

As Tori got back to the house, she heard the whine of the generator and saw the lights back on. Her mom and dad were standing outside on the front porch, phones held up to the sky.

"Still no signal," her mom said. "Do you think the cell towers are out?"

"Maybe," her dad replied. "I'll go up to the top of the hill and see if I can get any signal there."

"Dad," Tori came up next to him. She peered over his shoulder at his phone, which had an empty web page trying to load. "We were just up on the hill. It looks like there are fires around, and we could hear a fire truck siren."

"Well, we should probably go investigate." He went inside and got his truck keys, returning with a hopeful look on his face. "Shall we?" Tori and her dad got into the truck, Hudson and his mom staying behind with the dogs. The cracks in the driveway weren't too serious, and the truck went smoothly up their driveway. As they drove out to the main road, her dad kept checking his phone to get a signal. He even turned on the car's AM/FM radio, which they hardly ever listened to since they had music on their phone. The radio was static. He pushed buttons, switching to different presets. Still static.

"Hmmmm," he said in a slow and thoughtful tone.

The main road was dead quiet. He turned left towards the town, and before he got to the first bend in the road, a huge fallen tree blocked their path. "What do you think, Tori?" he asked. "Shall we go on a little adventure?"

She smiled nervously and nodded. He drove the truck slowly off the pavement and into the gravel so they could get around the tree. They continued down the road and could see more and more smoke columns floating up into the sky. Emergency sirens sounded in the distance, but they didn't see any other cars or people out.

As they came to the bridge of the nearby river, her dad came to a hard stop. The bridge had collapsed! It looked like the ground at the footing had given way, sliding right into the stream. "Well, I guess we won't be going that way," Tori said as she looked out the window. The house next to the road had also been severely damaged. The front wall had collapsed, and the roof was twisted. Noticing there wasn't a car in the driveway, she hoped the people had gotten out of harm's way.

They turned around and went back towards the house. As they came back to the driveway, her dad stopped the car, adjusting the dial on the radio. "Wait, there's a signal." Between the static, she could just make out an automated voice. He turned the volume up, and they listened to the message.

THIS IS THE EMERGENCY BROADCAST SYSTEM. THIS IS NOT A TEST. REPEAT. THIS IS NOT A TEST. SEVERE EARTHQUAKES NATIONWIDE. SEEK IMMEDIATE SHELTER AND AVOID RIVERS AND STREAMS. MULTIPLE DAMS HAVE COLLAPSED AND SEVERE FLOODING IS POSSIBLE. CITY AND HIGHWAY INFRASTRUCTURE HAS COLLAPSED. TRAVEL IS NOT ADVISED. REPEAT – TRAVEL IS NOT ADVISED. CELLULAR COMMUNICATION SYSTEMS ARE DOWN. POWER GRIDS ARE DOWN. EMERGENCY PROTOCOLS ARE IN PLACE. STAY HOME. STAY SAFE. THIS IS NOT A TEST. THIS IS THE EMERGENCY BROADCAST SYSTEM.

The message began to repeat itself. Her dad stifled some curse words as they drove back down the driveway. "Well, a good thing we turned around at the river Tori. Let's go tell your mom."

They got out of the car, and the dogs greeted them as if there wasn't a problem in the world.

"What did you find, sweetheart?" Her mom came up to them, hugging Tori.

"Well," he replied as he shut the truck door, "there's no phone signal and the bridge is out. I got an emergency alert on the AM radio in the car. It sounds like this is nationwide. Roads and bridges are out, and they aren't advising travel. It also confirmed that cell service is down and the entire power grid is down. They said we should just stay put. So, I guess that's what we'll do."

"Good thing we have the generator!" Tori replied. "But what about our friends? Do you think they're okay? How can we call them without phones?"

"We can't, Boo," Tori's mom used her childhood nickname. "We just

14

have to hope for the best right now and see what the day brings."

* * *

Tori and Hudson spent the morning cleaning up the house. With gloves, they carefully picked up the big chunks of broken glass, keeping the dogs outside so they wouldn't get it in their paws. They swept everything, worried the vacuum would overload the generator. Then they stood the bookshelves up, loading the books back on, and pushed the furniture back into place.

Without the TV, it was very quiet in the house. And no one talked either. What could anyone say? Everyone was worried but didn't want to say it out loud. Tori desperately wanted to call her friends, her aunts, uncles, and grandparents, but her phone didn't work. She wondered if their phones were working, and if they'd been trying to call and see if she was okay.

She wanted to drive and see if people were alright, but the bridge was out. She wanted to know what was going on, but they couldn't get any news on the radio or any cell service to get on the internet. Her dad would check the AM radio in the car from time to time, but it was the same message. Her mom looked equally worried, and her dad was pacing around, unable to hide his anxiety. Finally, he went outside to start cleaning up the trees that had fallen. "Just another day on the farm, right? There's always work to be done," he said as if trying to make things feel a little normal.

As the day went on, the unrelenting heat wave sent the temperatures soaring. They opened all the windows in the house, since the air conditioning wouldn't work on the generator.

"What is on the generator, Mom?" Hudson complained.

"The stuff that keeps you fed, alive, and safe," their mom grumbled

15

back.

Hudson began to bounce a ball against the wall. After he was tired of that, he flopped himself on and off the couch. Then he sighed and groaned, "I'm bored!"

"Why don't you go outside and check on your chickens?" Mom sent Hudson outside, grateful for some peace as she organized the mess their house had become after the earthquake. Tori stayed in, fiddling around on her phone, playing games that didn't need an Internet connection.

"Woah, Mom!" Hudson came rushing in, disrupting the freshly achieved stillness. "You gotta come outside! The sky is nuts!"

Tori and their mom got up and went to the front door. As they opened it, a blast of hot wind blew at them. Hudson ran into the front yard and looked up. The sky had turned a steel gray. The hot wind started to blow through the trees, shaking down limbs that had broken during the quake. Branches began to fall from the sky. "Hudson, Quick!" Tori called out. "Get back under the porch!"

From the porch, they watched the sky darken. In one area, the clouds began to move in a circular motion. In another, they came together to create shapes that looked almost like popcorn clouds. And the steel gray sky began to turn a creepy shade of green.

"Oh, crap," Mom called out in a sinking way. "I know what those clouds mean. Kids, get the dogs. We need to go inside. Now. I'm going to find your dad. Quick. Inside. Move!" She spoke with a force that gave no room for debate.

The hot wind stopped, and the whole world went into an eerie stillness as the kids and dogs raced inside. After this morning's earthquakes, no one wanted to mess around.

Their mom ran over to the woodpile where their dad had been

16

working, and the two came racing back to the house. The stillness had shifted, and a cold wind came and replaced the hot wind. Tori could feel the hair on her arms go up. Something was coming. As she thought about the circling clouds, only one thought came to her mind. Tornado.

"Hudson," she whispered to her brother, who was holding the dogs still. "I think that's a tornado you saw! How is this even possible? I thought tornadoes only happened out west!"

Hudson's eyes went wide. "Tori, what is going on? It kind of feels like the world is ending."

"It kind of does, doesn't it?" She held onto her brother in an unusual sign of sisterly affection as her parents came in and shut the door.

"Let's go into the bathroom, kids," her mom guided the four of them and the three dogs into the small downstairs bathroom. "I can't check the radar, but that cloud sure looks like a tornado. We'll be safe in here."

For a second time in one day, Tori's family huddled together. With no windows in the bathroom, they were safer, but had no idea what the sky was doing. They could hear the wind creaking and groaning through the trees. The sound grew louder, like a woosh of noise that didn't stop. It was almost like a train passing by, except it never passed. It just got louder and louder. They could hear big thumps as things hit the house. They huddled closer together, worried the roof might fly off or that the walls would collapse. The air felt electric, and the sound became so deafening that Tori covered her ears. Hudson began to cry, and their little dog shook like a leaf.

Then, when it seemed they couldn't bear another moment, the sound began to diminish. As quickly as they had started, the winds died down. The stillness became almost as loud as the noise of the wind, as they stood there in their bathroom in shock and disbelief.

"Let me go outside and check first," their dad volunteered. "You stay here for a minute."

He left the bathroom, and they heard him go out the front door. In a few minutes, he came back. "It's okay," he called out to them. "You can come out now. It is as safe as it's going to get."

They walked outside together and saw that what the earthquake had started, the tornado had finished. Trees were down everywhere. The chicken coop roof and doors had been completely blown off, but miraculously, the chickens were alive. They were wandering around the yard, looking a little dazed and confused, but safe.

As they stood there surveying the devastation, a cold wind blew in from the North. The heat of the day shifted instantly into a cold chill, causing them to shiver. The gray clouds opened up, and pouring rain began to fall.

"Well," Hudson said, picking up one of the chickens that had wandered over to him. "Today sure was a different kind of day."

* * *

Three

Reaching Out

Tori sat outside on their front porch as the sun began to set on what was perhaps the most frighteningly strange day of her life. But still, she was thankful. Her house was standing, and so was the barn, which had their horses and goats. They'd even been able to turn one of the horse stalls into a temporary chicken coop. They had a generator with plenty of fuel and a freezer and pantry full of food. Her mom was inside cooking dinner.

But Tori couldn't help but wonder how everyone else was doing. She looked at her phone one more time and sighed.

I should just stop looking at that, she said to herself. *It's not like I'm suddenly going to get a signal.* But she wasn't alone. Her mom had been looking at her phone all day, too. But there was no signal. Not even to make an emergency call. Her dad had some fancy app that could tie to a satellite system, but even that wasn't working. And the tornado had knocked down so many trees that there was no way they'd be able to drive anywhere anytime soon.

They were completely cut off from the rest of the world.

19

She kicked aimlessly at a toy ball as she stared out at the yard. She felt scared and worried. But mostly what she felt was helpless.

"Tori," her mom called. "Dinner time!"

The family had managed to pull the house back together to a kind of organized chaos. The table and chairs were still intact, and most of the broken things had been moved outside or stacked to the side of the living room. They sat down to a nice dinner of chicken, potatoes, and salad.

As Tori was filling her plate, her mom said, "Look, guys, we're all feeling a bit freaked out. I'm not going to try and tell you everything is going to be okay, because I don't know if it is." She paused.

"I want us to be honest about how we are feeling and to be okay to talk about it. But what I'll say is right now I'm feeling grateful. I'm grateful we are here and safe and have each other. So, let's take a deep breath and remember that at least. We've got each other. Especially you two," she looked at Tori and Hudson. "We're a team. We have to remember that. Together, we can get through anything the world throws at us. But only if we stick together. Just like your hockey team, Hudson."

Tori and Hudson rolled their eyes at each other over their mom's speech but nodded in agreement. If anything could bring a family together, an earthquake and a tornado all in one day could probably be the thing.

Their dad added, "I know everyone's probably wondering how your friends are doing. I'm still trying to see if I can get our phones tied to a sat system, but it doesn't work with the power grid out. And it's hard to do research when you can't get onto YouTube! But I'll keep working on it. And if not, hopefully the radio will send out some kind of update. Ever since the tornado, I haven't gotten any more messages. Just static."

After dinner, Tori and Hudson pulled out some books from the half-broken bookshelf. She picked up her dystopian novel about a post-apocalyptic America. She groaned out loud at the irony.

But something started to tickle her brain. It was an idea, but it wasn't quite coming to her mind. Something about a book. She kept reading, trying to let the idea roll around in her head to see if it would shake out. Then a lightbulb went off in her head.

"Of course! The Book!" she said out loud as she closed her book and jumped up. Her brother looked at her funny, his brown eyes wrinkling in confusion. "What's going on, Tori?" he asked, putting his own book down.

"The Book!" she cried. She looked into the next room where her parents were sitting at the table, and then quieted her voice as she turned back to Hudson. "The journal from the gnomes!" Hudson's eyes widened. "Come on, let's go up to my room."

The two of them ran upstairs to Tori's bedroom.

Last summer, Tori had met a charming gnome named Malcolm. He looked just like a garden gnome, but was as real as real could be. And Malcolm needed her help. He had discovered that Tori was a direct descendant of a powerful sorceress named Sorcha and that Tori had some of that magic still inside her. It wasn't the kind of magic that turned people into frogs, but she discovered that when she believed in herself, something magical happened inside her heart. It would light up and spread outward. And her heart magic made some pretty special things happen.

Malcolm asked her to go on a quest with his good friend Seamus to help an aging Phoenix die and be reborn. They went on a grand adventure through underground rivers across the Atlantic to Scotland. She helped save the King of the Gallywomps, creatures who lived deep below the surface of the Earth. Using magical Phoenix tears, she had cured a horrible skin condition that had caused him to be quite a grumpy king. And as a thank-you present, he had given her a magical stone that would warm anything it touched. He was the King of a place called the Land of Fire. Surrounded by huge volcanoes and lava, it was quite warm and toasty.

But the other present she got from her adventures was a magic journal. It had been a gift from the gnomes so that they could stay in touch wherever they were in the world. And that was the book that she had just remembered and was rushing to get from its secret hiding place.

"Hudson, close your eyes and turn away," she said, once they'd closed the bedroom door. "Why?" he complained.

"Look, I'll show you my journal, but I'm not going to show you where my secret hiding place is," she said sternly. "Do you want to see it or not?"

He closed his eyes and turned towards the door. Tori went behind her dresser and pulled out the small box she kept there. It had all the personal things she wanted to keep away from a nosy brother. She pulled the journal out and then put the box back.

"Okay, you can turn around now."

As Hudson turned around, he saw that Tori was holding a beautifully bound, bright blue journal with gold trim.

"Oohhhhhh," he breathed, reaching out to touch the journal. She pulled it away from him and sat on her bed. "Is that the journal you told me about? The one that sends messages to the gnomes?"

"Yes," Tori replied. "Here you can sit next to me, but DON'T TOUCH!" Hudson sat next to her on the bed, craning his head over to look at the journal. She opened it to where a gold tassel had marked the page.

As soon as she opened it, she could see there'd been loads of new writing since she'd last read it a month ago.

15 May
  Hey Tori, How's it going? The weather in Scotland has been really strange the last month. Write Soon!

Love, Malcolm

25 May

Tori, How are you wee lassie? Just wanted to check in. I was sailing in the rivers below the Atlantic this last week and things seem to be grumbling down here. It's like the walls are talking. It's quite strange. Have you noticed anything?

Regards, Seamus

2 June

Tori! Are you there? The gnome council just sent out an emergency notice to gnomes worldwide. Something is coming that is going to affect the whole world. The ancient books are calling it a Reset, but we don't know what that means. How are things at home?

Love, Malcolm

7 June

Tori, Please write us as soon as you can. We're worried about you, lassie! There were such huge earthquakes today. Some of the underground tunnels collapsed! Let us know you're safe.

A bit worried, Seamus

7 June

Tori, I just left the gnome council meeting. I'm sure you've experienced the same thing we just did - earthquakes, wind, and huge storms. So many trees down and homes smashed. From what we can tell many of the human cities are devastated. Our gnome network is reporting in from different countries as I write. I hope you find this journal soon. Please let us know you're okay.

Big Hugs, Malcolm

June 7th. That was today. "Oh my gosh, Hudson," Tori whispered, not believing what she was reading. "This didn't just happen here. It happened EVERYWHERE." Tori drew out the last word, reading again what the gnomes had written.

She quickly picked up a pen and wrote back to the gnomes.

June 7

Hey guys, I'm sorry I didn't see the journal until now. My last day of school was yesterday. We had huge earthquakes this morning and then a tornado! All in one day! We're safe, but our phones don't work, and we can't drive anywhere. How are you? Are you okay? Do the gnomes know what happened? Let me know if you know anything. We're all pretty worried.

Love, Tori

As she was writing, Hudson leaned closer, trying to read her message. After she'd finished and closed the journal, he looked at her with a serious expression on his face. "Tori," he said. "We HAVE to tell Mom and Dad about this. They need to know."

Tori stopped to think about this. On the one hand, she agreed with Hudson. They needed to know this had happened all over the world. But telling her parents about the gnomes and this journal also meant telling them how she had met them. Which meant telling them how she had lied last summer about going to camp and instead went with the gnomes on a quest to save the Phoenix.

"Hmmm," Tori said as she chewed on her lip.

"Come on, Tori," Hudson pulled on her sleeve. "This is important!"

Tori stood up from her bed and put the journal on her dresser. She hadn't made up her mind, but decided to go downstairs. "We will see what mood they're in," she said quietly as they walked down the wooden steps into the living room.

When they got downstairs, they didn't see their parents. Figuring they'd gone outside, Tori and Hudson walked out the front door towards the driveway. It was dark out now, but they saw their parents by the family's SUV. The door was open, and the cabin light was shining on their mom sitting in the driver's seat. Their dad was standing next to her. Walking over to them, they could hear the radio in the car turned up loudly.

There was a lot of static, but between the static, Tori heard a man's voice talking, his tone tight and a little panicky.

"Is that the news?" she called out to her dad. "Shhh!" he called back. "It's hard to hear." He motioned both of them over to the car. Hudson opened the passenger door so all four of them could listen to the man speaking on the radio.

Hello out there. This is Jered Rothstein talking to you from a small town outside Pittsburgh. If you're just tuning in, this is not an official broadcast or an official radio station. I'm with a group of HAM radio enthusiasts. We've managed to get a radio signal going across AM 1010. Repeat, that is 1010 on the AM dial. I've been talking with other people across the country. We are trying to get the news out to all of you out there wondering what's going on.

Maybe you've noticed that all the Emergency Broadcast systems are down. Maybe you're wondering when the power is coming back up. Maybe you've lost your home or are injured but can't get to the hospital.

Look, folks, we don't know everything, but here's what we do know. The massive earthquakes we felt today hit every single fault line in the United States. We aren't sure if it is worldwide, but we do know that they took out whole cities, the power grid, and most of the country's infrastructure. A few hours after, tornadoes sprang up all around the country, concentrating around major cities. Look, I'm no weatherman, but I can for sure say whatever storm that was, it was NOT normal. We heard stories that a tornado a half mile wide went through Washington D.C and destroyed the Capitol Building and many of the monuments. Another tornado devastated Philadelphia, Chicago, New York, and Miami.

I want to say this one more time. I am not an official with any government agency. As far as anyone can tell, there has been no word from any government organization – military or otherwise. Everything is dead quiet on the airwaves. There has been no organized military response to this crisis, or government news of any kind. It's like they up and vanished.

I will keep repeating this message and any more information we get at the top of each hour. If anyone out there has a HAM radio, please reach out and tell us what you know. We are listening. Initiate the call with CQ. Repeat, initiate the call saying CQ, and we'll get you into the network. We're on our own right now, so let's all work together.

Stay safe out there. Stay at home if you can. The roads are all blocked. If you can reach out to your neighbors, please lend a hand. Lots of people are hurt, injured, scared, or have lost their homes. But stay safe. We don't know what happened here, and we don't know what's coming. Signing off for now. Good luck.

The radio went back to static. Tori's mom turned the volume down and then shut off the car. Tears welled up in her eyes, and she wrapped both her kids in a fierce hug. They hugged her back, and their dad came over and wrapped all of them in his arms.

"Mom and Dad," Tori said, pulling out of the hug. "There's something I need to show you."

"Sure, honey," her mom said. "What do you need to show us? Is everything okay?"

"It's inside." Tori swallowed and took a deep breath. She had to tell her parents about the journal.

* * *

Tori ushered her parents into the living room, making them sit down on the couch while she went upstairs to get the journal. When she came down, Hudson was sitting in the side chair, curled up with their fluffy Aussie Shepherd.

"Are you okay, Tori?" Her mom asked, wondering if this conversation had something to do with the radio broadcast.

"Yeah, I'm fine," Tori quickly replied. "I mean, I'm not fine, like nobody's fine, but well, anyways, I just have something I think might help. But I have to tell you about something from last summer first."

"Sure, Tori, go ahead. We're all ears," her dad said in a comforting way.

Tori began, "Well, I don't know where to start. But I guess I'll start last summer at nature camp. Well, you see, I didn't actually end up going to nature camp. I kind of, well, I met these gnomes."

"Wait, what?" her mom interrupted her, alarmed. Tori knew she had started this off all wrong and looked to her brother with a grimace. He jumped in, "Hold on, Mom, listen to Tori. It's important."

Her mom was clearly agitated, but she stopped, allowing Tori to continue.

"I'm sorry, Mom and Dad. I know this is going to sound nuts. But last summer, a gnome, like a real live gnome, came to the farm. He had this ancient scroll and explained how we were descendants of a long line of magical people. He told me about this Phoenix, an actual magical Phoenix, that was dying. And if she didn't get help to be reborn, then the whole world would end. I mean, kind of like what it feels like is happening right now. And only people from that magical ancestor could help, so I kind of had to go, or who knows what could have happened."

Her parents looked like they were about to interrupt again, so she rushed on.

"I'm so, so sorry I didn't tell you because, well, I didn't think you'd let me go, and it was super important. And it just happened to be the same week as nature camp, but I didn't actually go to nature camp. I went with this gnome. His name is Malcolm and he's just the nicest guy, I mean gnome, you'd ever meet. And his friend Seamus, or Captain Douglas, actually, took us on this amazing boat through underground rivers to Scotland. That's where the Phoenix was, in Scotland. So, we went to Scotland and we met this magical horse, and he helped us escape these evil people, and then we found an enchanted village, and the Phoenix, and we saved her. I was totally safe the whole time."

"Scotland!!" her mom cut in. "Are you saying you went to Scotland instead of nature camp last summer! And with GNOMES? Tori, I don't know if I should believe you or worry that you hit your head and have a concussion. Either way, you lied to us, and that is so not okay. Honestly, if the world hadn't collapsed into a pile of rubble, you would be so grounded right now."

Tori looked down. She had felt so much guilt about this lie and holding it in all this time. She hadn't wanted to, and it had been eating her up for the past year. She almost felt relief at finally getting it out, even if it meant she'd be grounded.

"But," her mom continued, "Tell me why you have decided to tell us about this right now. You obviously have something to show us." She pointed at the book in Tori's hand.

"Of course. And Mom. I'm so sorry. Really, really sorry. But yeah, I do have something important to show you, and I think it could help." Tori took a deep breath, bringing her feelings back into some kind of control.

"So, Malcolm and Seamus are just the nicest and best gnomes ever. Anyways, after we helped the old Phoenix die and a new one get born, the new Phoenix flew all of us home. She flew me right back to nature camp, just in time to get picked up. I know it sounds crazy, but I'm telling the truth. Look. I have proof. You see, after I got back, Malcolm and Seamus gave me a present." She pulled out the journal.

"This is a magic journal they gave me so that we could keep in touch. They have another journal where they live, and when they write, it shows up in my journal, and the same goes when I write them. Here, look at the dates. I've been writing them back to last summer!"

Tori opened the journal and passed it over to her parents. The first entry started in August. She flipped the pages and showed them entries through the fall and winter. "And see, this is where I wrote, and this is where he wrote." She pointed out Malcolm's handwriting, which had attractive scrolls and refined lines.

"Mom, look at his handwriting," she continued. "There's no way I could make this up. You know I can't write that neatly. See? Here is my handwriting." She pointed to the messier print of her entries.

Her mom took the journal and began to go through the pages with her dad. Then they looked at the journal, its fine gold binding and decorative trim. It didn't look like some sort of magic trick or gimmick book. "Where could she have gotten this?" she mused out loud.

"And look, Mom!" Tori took the journal back, eager to convince her parents she wasn't making this up. "Look at the entries from the past two weeks!" She flipped to the page that showed the writings from

Seamus and Malcolm about the earthquakes. "Read this, Dad! It's just like what we heard on the radio."

Her parents read through the entries, ending with Tori's from just an hour before.

"I don't know what to say, Tori." Her mother was very confused. "I mean, today is such a crazy day. I am almost tempted to believe you, but I just don't know how. It all seems a bit too much. Gnomes. Magic journals. Phoenixes." She sighed. "Look, I'm really upset about last summer and you lying to us, but at the moment that seems like the least of our worries."

Tori waited in silence. She'd done what she said she was going to do. Now she had to see if her parents would believe her.

Then, as her mom held the journal open, words began to appear on the page. She looked at her husband in disbelief.

8 June

Tori! I am so glad to hear from you! And SOO glad you're okay. It's early morning here, and I don't know much more than yesterday, but stand by! The gnome council is meeting soon. I'm just so glad you're safe, my friend. Will write as soon as I know more.

Lots of love, Malcolm

"Tori, I don't know what to say," her mom said, working out each word. "Except I guess I'm glad? Glad that you happen to have this journal and have friends who are gnomes. They seem to know more about what's going on than all the humans combined right now."

Tori gave her mom and dad a big hug. "I'm so sorry I didn't tell you guys. I just didn't know how."

They hugged her back. "It's okay. I can understand. I don't think we'd have believed you," her mom replied.

Her dad added, "Honestly, I only think we'd even think such a thing was possible because we had a day like today."

He pulled back and took Hudson into a family hug.

"Look, kids," he said after a long embrace, "It's getting late, and it has been a long day for all of us. Let's get you two off to bed. There's a lot we don't know right now, but you're both safe, and that's what counts for me."

"Maybe tomorrow morning will bring some good news," their mom added, sending them upstairs to brush their teeth. "If you want, we can all snuggle in bed together tonight. I think it might make us all feel a little safer." Even though Tori hadn't slept with her parents in years, she agreed. That seemed like a good thing to do after a day like today.

Their parents let the dogs out and checked on the generator. They came upstairs shortly after Hudson and Tori. Exhausted, they all crashed into the king-size bed. Parents, kids, and dogs all snuggled into a giant pile of comfort and love.

Thankfully, the night brought no more storms or quakes. Hudson woke up from a scary dream, but his mom held him tight, and he fell back to sleep. Tori dreamed of her friends, Malcolm and Seamus, and the beautiful Phoenix they had met last summer.

* * *

* * *

Four

The Great Reset

As the sun began to peek into the bedroom window, Tori woke up to the sound of the generator sputtering. She sat up, uncurling herself from her dog Maggie, who was lying between her and her mom. "Dad," she called out and then noticed he'd already left. The generator stopped, and the light in the hallway went out. "I guess the power's still off," Tori said out loud.

After a moment, she heard the generator firing back up and the light turning on again. Her dad must have been refilling the fuel. Tori wondered if he'd heard any more news about the earthquakes and tornadoes. Yawning, she got out of bed and made her way downstairs.

Her dad was out by the truck, listening to the radio broadcast.

"Any news, Dad?" she called out as she walked towards him.

He nodded at her as he turned off the radio and shut the door. "Yeah," he sighed, walking back to the house. "Not good, I'm afraid. Let's go inside and get your mom and brother, and I can share what I heard."

Tori's dad poured himself a big cup of coffee and made her a small cup with extra milk. She'd started drinking coffee this spring. Her

33

parents didn't mind as long as it was half coffee and half milk. As her mom and brother came downstairs, they made themselves some tea, then convened at the kitchen table.

Her dad looked somber as he delivered the news.

"It's hard to even put into words, guys. Entire cities are," he stopped, overcome with emotion. "They're gone."

Everyone's eyes widened as Hudson whispered, "What do you mean gone?"

"The earthquakes. The lands at the edge of tectonic plates completely crashed into the ocean, like the west coast of North and South America. California, Chile, Alaska. Gone. Like apocalypse gone." Images of apocalypse movies flashed into Tori's mind. Great tears in the earth swallowing buildings. Bridges collapsing into the water.

"But what about here? We aren't on a tectonic plate, are we?" They'd learned about this in school this year, how the Earth's crust had plates that moved and shifted above the volcanic magma underneath.

"No, you're right, Tori. We don't live near a tectonic plate," her mom said. "Rob, did they say anything about why we had all these earthquakes?"

"The guy on the radio connected with some geologists," he explained. "I guess the country, really the world, is full of inactive fault lines. But sometimes, if there's great pressure on the Earth's crust, they can reactivate to help relieve that pressure. That's what happened yesterday. The Earth had a huge shift on the plates, and all the fault lines around the world shook in response. There are fault lines in the middle of the country, near St. Louis and Chicago, and along the Rocky Mountains. They also run all along the East Coast, where we live, from Maine to Florida."

"Wow," Tori's jaw dropped. "So, this really was everywhere."

"Yeah, I'm afraid so," her dad continued. "And the tornadoes, they don't understand why those happened, but massive storms went all across the country. They just took everything out—power grids, cell towers, roads, buildings, military bases, and parts of cities. And the government collapsed with the earthquakes and the storms. I mean, sure, there's no way they could have prepared for something like this, but still. Our government is completely silent. No response at all. It's weird. Like everyone just up and went home."

He took a long pause, letting the words sink in, then continued. "So, we're all just on our own. To figure out what to do next."

Hudson moved closer to his mom, a look of worry painted on his face as he bit his lip and creased his brow.

"The guy on the radio said people are calling it 'The Great Reset.' Some say it's a religious Armageddon. Others say it's climate change, and it's what we get for not taking care of the planet. In this house, we believe in science. The weather has been getting crazier each year. But I don't know what to say about the earthquakes. Honestly, I don't know what to think. But I do know that we've got each other. We've got the generator and enough fuel, food, and water to last a month. And you kids are safe. That's all that matters right now."

Tori's parents had always been into the idea of homesteading and making sure they could be self-sufficient. Since they lived on a farm far from cities, the power sometimes went out for a day or two, so they had a generator. They also kept an emergency supply of food and water to last a month. Tori realized just how lucky she was. Most people didn't have these emergency supplies.

"Mom," she asked, thinking about her friends, "What about Madi? Or Jessica? Or Grandpa and Grandma? I don't think they have food supplies like we do. Are they going to be okay? Are they okay now?" Tori was often thinking about others, wanting to share whatever she had with anyone who didn't have enough.

Tori looked at her mom and saw that her eyes were starting to swell up with tears. And then Tori's tears started to come too. "Mom, is it that bad?"

"I don't know, sweetie." She wrapped Tori in a big hug as the tears started to flow down her cheeks. "But I think yes, it might be that bad."

* * *

After a lot of hugging and crying, their mom sent Tori and Hudson outside to do some farm chores. She and their dad needed to have some grown-up conversations.

As Hudson opened the temporary coop door to let the chickens out for the day, he asked Tori, "What do you think's going to happen? Are you scared?"

Tori was scared, but tried to sound confident to her little brother. "Nah, I'm not scared. Look, I've read loads of books about the end of the world and stuff. The one thing you can't be is scared, Hudson. We have to stick together and be brave, no matter what happens. That's how we survive."

"But what if we run out of food?" he asked.

"We live on a farm!" She pulled out some fresh eggs from the chicken's nest box. "We've got loads of food!"

"Well," Hudson nodded, but then thought of another fear, "what if people come and try and take our food?"

Tori paused. She knew that was something to be worried about and guessed her parents might be talking about that right now in the house. But then Tori remembered her adventure with the gnomes last summer. She had met bad men who were trying to capture the Phoenix. But she and the gnomes outwitted them with the help of the magical horse Ahearn.

36

She had met a king who was very sick and miserable and made everyone in his kingdom greedy and miserable, too. But when she healed his sickness with Phoenix tears, his good nature came back, and the kingdom prospered again.

She remembered what the Phoenix had taught her. When she believed in love and goodness, magical things could happen.

"Look, Hudson," she turned and looked square at him, eye to eye, "We're all scared. And the people who don't have a farm or electricity are probably even more scared than us. But we can't focus on the scary possibilities. We have to try and be positive. Being positive makes more positive. Being negative makes more negative. If people come, we'll share the best we can. We'll try and help each other, because that's what we should do. And if they get mean, then we'll just outsmart them!"

Tori stood up tall and determined to practice what she said. To be positive to make more positive. The heroes in her books never gave up when things got tough.

"We just have to be brave and keep going, Hudson. One step at a time," she said, and went to feed the horses their morning grain.

Hudson stood up tall and followed her, also determined to be brave.

* * *

When Tori and Hudson returned to the house, their parents were waiting for them with determined looks on their faces. They told both of them that under no circumstances were they to leave the farm property. But their dad was going to take the tractor out later to see if he could check in with neighbors.

"We figured it could go more off-road than the truck," their dad told them. "If I can help anyone out with repairs, I will, but I am not bringing anyone back to the farm. And I don't want you going anywhere either. Keeping you kids safe and fed is my number one priority."

Their mom was going to go through the house and make an inventory of all they had food-wise and come up with a plan for menus and meals. "No grocery store runs for us kids. No Chik-Fil-A or Starbucks mochaccinos. We've got to pull together and make do with what we have. We will use this Great Reset to get creative with our cooking!" she finished, trying to sound enthusiastic.

Hudson and Tori both agreed, also mustering some enthusiasm to support their parents. They tried to keep that positive attitude when their mom sent them up to their rooms to clean and organize their closets and supplies.

But as Tori walked upstairs, she remembered the journal. *That's right!* she thought, *Malcolm was going to write me back after the gnome council!*

She rushed into her room, all thoughts of organizing her closet forgotten as she retrieved the blue book.

8/9 Who knows? June

Dear Tori, the world's gone topsy turvy, hasn't it? I'm so glad you're safe and that you don't live in a city. It seems like people in cities are not doing well AT ALL. Stay on your farm if you can!

The gnome council met. A gnome from China found an ancient book that talked about different Epochs, or eras of time. The book prophesied this! Here's exactly what it said:

"And a time of great stress and strain in humanity will come, and the world will also feel that strain. The Earth will crack and buckle, and great cities will fall. Storms will sweep the seas and the forests, washing away the old ways of greed and power. Governments will crumble, and the old will look to the young to lead them into the future. From the ashes of the Phoenix, a new epoch will be born. A time of peace and harmony. A time of love and light. And the young will lead the way."

Crazy, right? Look, Seamus and I are trying to figure out how to come see you. The underground rivers are a mess with the earthquakes, but good ol' Captain Douglas has never met a river he can't navigate. Hold on! We're coming!

So much love, Malcolm

Tori had learned last year that the magical Phoenix dies and is reborn every 500 years or so. Was it just a coincidence that the new Phoenix was born last year, and this prophecy mentioned a Phoenix? She decided to write back and ask Malcolm.

Malcolm, that will be so great if you can come. I told my parents about you and the journal, but I don't know if they believe me. Do you think it's a coincidence that the prophecy mentioned a Phoenix? And the old people asking the young to lead!?!? I'll believe that when I see it!

Hope to see you soon, Love, Tori

Tori sat with the words of the prophecy as she casually attempted to clean her room. The people on the radio were calling this the Great Reset. And the prophecy kind of did, too. But it almost talked about it like this was a good thing. But how could all this destruction be a good thing? She wanted to talk to Malcolm, not just write back and forth. She hoped they'd be able to find a way here. She had so many questions.

* * *

* * *

Five

Coming Together

Tori spent an hour in her room, cleaning up what had fallen in the quake and putting away her clothes. Then she decided to tell her brother about the new message in the journal. He'd probably laugh at the idea that adults would listen to kids instead of telling them what to do.

She went and knocked on his door. She'd made him do it for her, so she had to follow the same rules. "Who is it?" he called out.

"Good grief, Hudson, who do you think it is?" she rolled her eyes. "Can I come in?"

"I guess so." He opened his door, and she walked into the bomb cyclone that was his bedroom. A tackle box full of rocks and fossils lay open on the floor. His feather collection and a dozen books were scattered across his dresser, and his clothes had escaped the hamper and were all over the floor.

"What a mess, Hudson," she scolded, "did the earthquake do this, or does it always look this bad?" He scrunched up his nose at her. "Whatever, Tori. Your room is way worse. At least all my fossils are organized," he pointed to his box. "You just leave everything all over

41

the place."

Tori rolled her eyes again and found an open spot on his bed to show him the journal. "Malcolm wrote me back. He said they found a prophecy that predicted this exact thing would happen. And here's what's crazy. It said the old will look to the young to lead. Can you even imagine?"

Not everyone would know it by first looking at Hudson's wild blonde hair and oversized hockey jerseys, but he was a very bright and observant boy. He often noticed things that no one else saw. He made connections and observations about people that would astound his parents. But everyone still treated him like a little kid who didn't know anything. "Yeah, right," he said sarcastically. "They'd never in a million years let us lead. Hey, let me see the prophecy!"

As she opened the journal to show him, she saw Malcolm had written back already. It was one quick sentence.

There are no such things as coincidences, my dear. See you soon.
XX -M

"So, you think I'll get to meet them?" Hudson asked. A part of him still didn't know if he believed Tori, but he was always open to an adventure. And after what had happened in the last two days, anything seemed possible. "What are they like?"

"Well," Tori began, closing her eyes as she remembered her two gnome friends. "Malcolm is incredibly polite. He's got a British accent, and Seamus has more like a Scottish accent. They are both pretty short!" Tori held her hand about three feet off the ground. "And that's with their hats! They wear big pointy hats and have long beards." She pulled her hand down from her chin to her belly button to show just how long their beards were. "Oh, and Malcolm loves jewelry and colorful things. I bet you'd like him because he loves rainbows and crystals as much as you. He's also really smart, but so is Seamus! I bet you'll like Seamus, too, because he LOVES adventure. He is an amazing captain on his boat, and he steered us through some really fast rivers."

"Ooh, that sounds cool. I like the water!" Hudson added. "Are they the same age? How old are they?"

"I don't know, actually," Tori replied, tapping her finger on her chin as she thought. "I think gnomes live a lot longer than people. They are magical after all. But it does seem like Malcolm is younger than Seamus. But he can't be that young, because he seems to be on this gnome council, and knows all this stuff about prophecies and history books. Oh, and he loves to eat. Like when we were traveling, he was always planning our next meal. He's super nice. And he's funny, too."

Looking at her with both hope and fear in his eyes, Hudson said, "Well, I hope they can get here with all the underground rivers collapsing. I wonder if they have any more of a plan than our parents do? They seem to know a lot of things humans don't know about." He jumped up excitedly. "We should tell Mom and Dad they're coming! And about the prophecy!"

Tori agreed, and journal in hand, they went off in search of their parents.

Their dad had gone off exploring the neighborhood with his trusty red tractor, and their mom was downstairs sitting on the couch reading a book.

"Mom, you're reading?" Tori looked shocked. "You NEVER have time to read!"

Her mom laughed. "Well, Tori, to conserve fuel for the generator, we can't run the laundry machines or the vacuum, and I don't have internet for my phone. We may end up with a lot of dirty clothes and a messy house before too long, but for now, I think I earned a moment to just sit and relax. It's been a bit stressful, don't you think?"

"For sure, Mom!" Hudson chimed in, "Good for you. It's good to take care of your needs sometimes."

Their mom laughed, hearing her own words of advice coming back to her.

Tori sat down next to her mom and opened the gnome's journal. "Mom, check this out. The gnomes are coming to visit! And they found an ancient prophecy that predicted all of this! I think they've got a plan to help!"

Mom sighed. "Well, kids, our government has clearly failed us. At this point, I'm more than happy to put the fate of the world into the hands of some magical creatures and an ancient prophecy. We can't be any worse off. Plus, who doesn't love gnomes, right?"

Tori grinned. "Honestly, Mom, you're going to love them. They are so nice. And they seem to know about lots of things we don't know about. I bet they even understand why we had these earthquakes!" Tori jumped up, excited. "I'm going to see if I can find some of their favorite foods, so we can make them a nice meal when they get here!" She was sure Seamus would find a way, and he would get there faster than any plane could fly.

"Sounds good, Tori. And if you and your brother want to put together dinner for all of us, I won't complain. Mommy needs to just sit here for a bit." Their mom opened her book and looked out the window at the downed trees and the collapsed chicken house. "I'll get back to being a grown-up soon enough."

As the day went on, Tori kept checking the journal, but there had been no more news. Did that mean they were already on their way along the rivers? Had Seamus found a passage through the collapsed tunnels?

Had the gnome council had more meetings?

She had so many questions but no good answers. She was restless, but wasn't feeling very useful either. Their mom tried to get them to clean the yard together, but she and her brother just started fighting. Tori just couldn't focus on anything today, and her brother's constant chatter was annoying her.

Hudson was also annoyed with Tori. He was excited at the idea of meeting the gnomes, but he was more concerned about the damage to the farm. His farm was his everything, and he knew every tree and bird that lived there. He knew where all the birds' nests were, where the frogs lived, and where the deer liked to sleep during the day. He was devastated to see all the damage from the earthquake and storms. He kept asking Tori to help him with replacing a bird nest or dragging some limbs around to clear the path, but her mind was elsewhere.

Frustrated, he went off and started doing things himself. Dressed in knee-high mud boots, shorts, and a rainbow tie-dye shirt, Hudson marched around the farm trying to put things back in order. The things that were too big for him to move, he took note of so he could tell his dad about them later.

Eventually, he got tired and hungry and went back to the house. Tori was on the front porch and looked up when he came up the steps. "Guess what?" Her excitement made her forget that she'd been mad at him hours before. "The gnomes will be here tomorrow! They wrote me!"

"Cool," he said. "So, they found a way to get through the rivers?"

"Yeah, I guess so. Anyways, Mom made dinner. It's almost ready."

They went inside and ate dinner with their parents. Their dad had returned from his expedition to the neighbors.

He had gotten to four neighbors' houses that day. Luckily, three were okay. The people were safe and not hurt. Two of the houses had been really damaged, but they had camping gear and a stream nearby with fresh water. When they asked about the fourth house, he got quiet for a moment. He told them that the tornado had gone right through the house.

He spoke quietly, "I used the tractor to help me," he paused, choking up. Then he resumed with a forceful gravity, "I laid them to rest under an old oak tree."

They didn't ask any more. They understood. After that, they ate in silence.

It was a somber night in their house as they realized that not everyone was as lucky as they were. Each family was trying the best they could, and some had suffered more than others. Tori hoped the gnomes had a plan, but she asked her dad if he'd keep going out to help the neighbors. He said he had to do some repairs at their farm tomorrow, but he promised he'd keep going out to help. "It's not like work is going to call me and ask why I haven't logged in today."

Tori went back to sleep in her own bed that night, though Hudson was still scared and wanted to sleep with his parents. But she had restless dreams and woke up tired and irritable. The bright summer sun annoyed her as she blinked, reaching for her glasses.

But as she put them on, she remembered, 'The gnomes! They will probably be here any minute!'

She jumped up to brush her teeth and change out of her pajamas. She remembered that Malcolm had a funny habit of turning up in places she least expected. She didn't want to find him there in her bedroom when she was still in pajamas.

She pulled on jean shorts and a purple top, brushed her hair, and pulled it back into a ponytail. Once she was dressed, she went down to the kitchen to get herself some coffee.

And sitting on the kitchen counter, checking out the fruit basket, were Malcolm and Seamus!

"Malcolm! Seamus!" she cried out, running over to her friends. "It is SO good to see you!" She wrapped both of them in one giant hug. Their hats squished together, and Seamus struggled against getting squeezed so hard.

"There, there, lassie," he called out, his voice muffled in her arms. "No need to squeeze us to death before we've even had breakfast."

Tori laughed and released them from her bear hug, and then gave each one a smaller, more gnome-sized hug. "I'm sorry, dear Captain Douglas," she winked at him, "I didn't mean to ruffle your beard so much."

He blushed a bit and grinned, his blue eyes twinkling above his beard. "Not to worry, not to worry." He stood up, stretched, and yawned. "But my word, we've had a long trek here! I don't suppose you could be spared a cup or two of tea, could ye?"

"Absolutely!" Tori went over to the tea cupboard. "We have some coffee already made if you'd like some." She turned around and saw Malcolm scowl.

"Coffee," he wrinkled his round nose, "My dear Tori, when did you start drinking coffee? I thought you were a tea girl like us?"

"Oh, I still like tea," she smiled, "But when I turned 11, my dad told me I could have coffee in the morning, too." She grinned at them. "He said I'd gone to bed one night and woke up a grump monster the next, and coffee was the only cure." She laughed good naturedly. It was true that recently she liked to sleep a lot later than she used to, and there was very little that could wake her up.

Tori turned the electric kettle on and found the smallest cups she could find for the gnomes. As the water boiled, the two gnomes began to pull out some fruits from the basket on the counter and made other suggestions about what kind of breakfast they'd enjoy. As the list continued to grow from toast and fruit to sausages, eggs, and anything else they could think of, she wondered how long they'd been traveling.

"You seem quite hungry. Was it a long trip?" she asked.

"Oh, you would not even believe it!" Seamus proclaimed as Malcolm nodded. "The rivers are a right mess. We had to backtrack and detour to find a way through. There were so many collapsed tunnels and raging rapids. The North Passage is wilder than I've ever seen it."

Malcolm nodded seriously, and then grinned mischievously, "And the water was positively RAGING! It was full speed and then some. Captain Douglas really earned his stripes last night, and that's saying something. But once we got past the idea that we might die at any moment, it was EXHILARATING!" He said the last word quite loudly, and as he did, a voice came from the next room.

"Who's that? What was exhilarating?"

It was Hudson, and he came running into the kitchen to see who was there.

"Wow! Tori, they ARE real!" Hudson stopped short, staring at the two gnomes sitting on the edge of the kitchen counter.

"Pleased to make your acquaintance, Hudson," Malcolm said politely, tipping his red hat. "May I introduce myself. I am Malcolm, at your service. And this is Captain Douglas, riverboat captain extraordinaire."

"Ay, please to meet you, Master Hudson," Seamus said quite seriously, and then winked. "But my friends just call me Seamus."

Hudson stared in silence for a moment, realizing the gnomes his sister had told him about were now in his kitchen. "It is nice to meet you, too. What was exhilarating?" he asked again.

"Oh, yes!" Seamus replied, "Why, our trip here was quite the adventure indeed. We can tell you all about it over some breakfast. We're so hungry we might fade to nothing any minute."

Tori had by now pulled together enough food to feed the starving gnomes, grateful her dad had already cooked up some eggs and sausages that morning. Once everyone had their tea and coffee, the four sat down to a feast of buttered toast, yogurt, scrambled eggs, sausages, and strawberries.

* * *

The North Passage

***

Six

The Prophecy

Malcolm and Seamus devoured the food like they hadn't eaten in days, which surprised Tori. They were always so regular on mealtimes when she traveled with them last summer.

"So?" Tori asked, starting to wonder if they were ever going to tell the story. "What's going on, Malcolm?"

Malcolm nodded as he swallowed a bit of toast. "Sorry, my dear," he gulped, "it was quite a wild ride to get here on the North Passage. Seamus warned me about it, but I truly didn't know what I was getting into."

Seamus knowingly winked at them while Malcolm continued. "But it was the only way! All the cross rivers are blocked! Tunnels blocked, raging rapids, and huge boulders that Seamus barely avoided. My word! It was quite something to be sure!"

For a moment, Malcolm looked distressed by the experience, but then his smile reappeared from under his beard, and his eyes twinkled as he looked at Hudson. "You're going to love it, wee man!"

Hudson snapped to attention. "Wait, what do you mean? Are we going to go on this North Passage?"

Seamus chuckled at Malcolm, "There you go again, getting ahead of your story. Why don't you start from the beginning?"

"Yes," Tori demanded. "What do you know about any of this?"

Malcolm grinned sheepishly, drinking a sip of tea, and told them all he knew.

"It's quite a curious thing, this book that had this prophecy. I think I told you it was found by our gnome brothers in China, but it isn't Chinese. It is in the language of our ancient kin from the far North. They are wise mystics, shrouded in ancient mysteries and lore. Rarely seen, even by the kind folk, but they are wise. So wise," Malcolm said with an air of reverence.

"The book contained references to all the great wars of humans, long before they happened. But not just human conflict, it spoke of natural disasters, too. It didn't have specific dates, but the council cross-referenced it against our histories. It foretold huge meteor strikes, major floods, volcanic eruptions, everything! It's a book that calls out everything that ever happened and ever will happen! And it predicted this exact moment!"

Tori got chills thinking about a book, or rather, the wise mystics who wrote the book, who knew such horrible things were going to happen. What a burden it would be to know about all these catastrophes.

"Is it always the bad things that it wrote about?" Hudson asked curiously. "Are there ever good things that happen?"

"Quite right, Hudson," Seamus replied. "Quite right, indeed. Come now, Malcolm, it's not all doom and gloom."

"Of course, of course," Malcolm agreed. "It also told of great moments of human achievement, like the artists of the Renaissance, the great Greek Philosophers, and the wise Egyptian Architects. It told the whole story and painted a picture of it all like it was a great tapestry, with ups and downs through time. It's just that right now, well maybe we could say it is a bit of a down."

"You got that right!" Hudson exclaimed. "A big down."

Tori's mind was spinning with questions. "What did the book say came after this? What happens next?"

Malcolm bit his lip. "Well, you see, that's the problem. The book ends right after the prophecy."

Hudson looked alarmed. "Ends? What do you mean, ends? Are you saying this is the end of the world?" He put his fork down, suddenly losing his appetite.

"Well, no," Malcolm began, "not necessarily. The book didn't start at the beginning of the world. It started at the beginning of this Age. There were ages, or epochs, before this one. The Atlanteans, the Lemurians, and don't forget the Dinosaurs. They weren't as dumb as your science books say. The world is much older than this book, and it will surely go on long after today." He paused and then said quietly, "I hope."

Tori ignored his last comment and asked her next question. "Okay, so we don't know what comes after the prophecy, but is there someone we can ask? Who are these people who wrote it? Or sorry, did you say they are gnomes, too? Are they still around somewhere? If they know everything that's going to happen, can't we ask them what's going to happen now? Maybe there's another book somewhere?"

Malcolm grinned, "Precisely, my dear Tori. That is exactly what we are hoping to do. And no, they aren't gnomes. They are actually elves, from the far North. And well, you may laugh, but they do in fact live…. Well, take a guess…"

"Northern elves?" Hudson crinkled his face in thought. "Wait, are you saying, are these elves, like the ones that live at the NORTH POLE? Like Santa's elves?"

Malcolm nodded slowly.

"You're kidding," Tori groaned. "Are you telling us that not only are Santa's elves real but that they are wise mystics who write books of prophecy?"

Hudson gave Tori a sharp look. "Of course Santa's elves are real, but I thought they made toys."

Malcolm chuckled, "Yes, Hudson, they are as real as you and me. And only non-believers," he looked pointedly at Tori, "which I didn't think you were, Miss Victoria, think otherwise." She looked down sheepishly, realizing if gnomes were real, then elves must be real, too.

He continued, "But it is not as simple as the stories say. Many elves live in the North, at the top of the world. They are hidden far away from man in deep, vast underground crystal cities. But they are not all toy makers, just as not all humans are builders or bakers. There are many elves there, more than I think you might imagine. We gnomes have good relations with them. Not exactly sending Christmas cards each year, but we're all friendly when we bump into each other. But the ones who wrote this book are the mysterious ones.

We call them the Weavers, though no one can quite remember why. But no gnome has seen a Weaver in, well, the council can't even recall the last time anyone saw a Weaver. Which was why it was all so exciting to find one of their books in our libraries!"

Seamus interrupted Malcolm at this point, a mischievous grin on his wrinkled face. "Ay, Malcolm is right. No one has seen them, but we think it's high time for that to change. We aim to go find these mysterious mystics and have a good word with them!"

Tori could sense adventure and excitement in Seamus' voice and excitedly asked, "Do you want us to come? Is that why you came here?"

"Ay lassie!" Seamus exclaimed. "That's exactly why we came!"

Malcolm interrupted now, trying to bring some calm back to the moment. "But it's not like we are going off on some crackpot adventure, this is what the prophecy foretold. It said the children will lead the way. Not the adults, or the gnomes, or even the Phoenix you helped last year. The children. And so, the council all agreed that we needed to have children to help us find the Weavers."

Hudson had been listening intently to the conversation. "Well, of course, children will lead the way. It's not like adults can go to the North Pole or meet Santa's elves. Everybody knows that!"

Malcolm laughed, "You are quite right, my friend. Quite right. The North Pole is protected with plenty of enchantments to keep humans out, especially grown-ups. But Santa's always had a soft spot for children. You're still so pure and innocent. I'm sure it's no coincidence that the prophecy said the children will lead the way, and then it's only children that could go to the North Pole."

Hudson squinted his eyes at Tori, sending her a silent *'I'm smarter than you are.'*

Seamus laughed, seeing the exchange between the children, and said enthusiastically, "So what do you say, shall we get packing?"

"Wait, hold on a minute," Hudson said seriously. "We can't just go off to the North Pole. What about Mom and Dad? Do you think they're going to be cool with this? And is it just the four of us that are supposed to be going to save the world?"

Malcolm sobered, "Oh, yes, we shall need to explain the importance of this mission to your parents, and why it has to be you and not them. But it's not just us, my dear Hudson. There are gnomes around the world reaching out to other children as we speak, asking them this same question. Will you help us go find the Weavers? The world has collapsed and needs our help!"

Tori remembered being frightened before the quest for the Phoenix. She remembered feeling that there must be someone else who could do this, or that she should play it safe. She wondered if Hudson was thinking the same thing right now, though he was always ready to do crazy things. Shoot, he probably already had his bag packed.

But she had learned something from her last adventure. Sometimes things come along and ask you to step up and have courage. We can't hope someone else will do it. We have to do it. Even if we're afraid.

She looked over at Hudson to see if he seemed scared. He was bouncing up and down in his seat. She groaned. "Are you sure that BOTH of us have to go?" she asked Malcolm. "Maybe it should just be me, like last time." The idea of being in a boat with her brother for more than an hour sounded horrible.

"Oh, come now, Miss Tori," Seamus scolded her, "and let wee Hudson miss out on all the fun? Of course, you both need to go! You never know when his brave courage and wild spirit might come in handy."

"It's more likely to get us killed," Tori groaned, but she knew she couldn't leave him behind. As much as he annoyed her, they were both in this mess together.

"Yeah, Tori," Hudson stuck his tongue out at her, "My courage and bravery are going to come in way handier than your boringness." He ducked under the table just as she reached out to hit him. "See!" he peeked his head up from the floor! "And I'm super quick."

"Good grief," Tori groaned. "Well, I guess that settles it. Now all we need to do is go talk to Mom and Dad."

* * *

Seven

The North Passage

The conversation with Mom and Dad went about how Tori would have expected it to go. Two kids ask their parents to go with a pair of gnomes to the North Pole by way of underground rivers to find a lost, mystical tribe of elves. It was a mix of disbelief, worry, fear, disbelief, and worry again.

But there is something about having two gnomes in your living room that can begin to shift even the most rigid of minds. Then, add that they'd gone through two days of the most bizarre experiences of their lives, Tori's parents began to cave on the idea of them going on this little adventure.

Naturally, her parents wanted to go instead to keep their kids safe. Malcolm explained how only children could travel to the North Pole, and why it was so important to find the Weavers. They worried Tori and Hudson would be in danger traveling the underground rivers. Tori told them how expertly Seamus had guided her in the rivers around Iceland and Scotland. She talked of how Malcolm had kept her safe, fed, and warm. Gnomes are quite gentle and caring as magical creatures go, and there's honestly no better traveling companions if you're about to go on an adventure.

The discussions went on for an hour, but slowly Malcolm and Seamus were able to address the many concerns their mom and dad had about their safety. Nothing felt very safe right now, anyway, as they had no power, cell phones, or connection with the outside world.

And honestly, as brave as Hudson was at first, it was good for him to hear these details. He'd done some traveling for hockey and on vacations, but he'd never been away from home alone, unless you counted a sleepover at a friend's house. As much as he was putting on a brave face, he had a lot of anxiety about leaving the farm. His mind went to all the things that could go wrong. It was nice to hear that Malcolm and Seamus had so much experience traveling on these rivers. Seamus told them about his boat, how sturdy it was, and all the provisions he'd packed. He had food for at least a week, and he was sure it would take less than that.

"But how will we know if you're okay?" their mom asked. "Our phones don't work, and there's just so much uncertainty right now. Isn't there any way for you to keep in touch? Hudson's never been away from home before. I'm not okay with him being away for a whole week without any way to check on him."

"It's just a quick out and back," Seamus reassured them. "All we need to do is get the children there, find the Weavers, get the answers, and come home. Quick as a blink."

Mom had a sixth sense for seeing through people's words. She could tell Seamus wasn't telling her about all the dangers of the rivers. "There must be some way for you to let us know they are okay while you're gone. Don't you have some kind of magic?"

Suddenly, Malcolm laughed out loud. "Of course we do! Silly me, what was I thinking? We have the books!"

Malcolm pulled out the red journal he used to write to Tori. "Here you go, Mrs. Johnson. We can use these books to write to you. This one is mine," he handed the book to her, "and we will take Tori's with us. That way, you can write to the children, and they can write to you."

Hudson exhaled a sigh of relief as his mom opened the book to look at the messages. He hadn't realized how worried he'd been about being away from home until his mom had asked about him calling. But the books solved that problem. Suddenly, it sounded more like an adventure.

Tori looked around, seeing that her parents had asked all their questions. "So, Mom? Dad?" she asked. "Can Hudson and I go start packing?"

Dad had a look of dread on his face. He was very protective of his children and loved them fiercely. It almost looked like he was going to say no, when Mom put her hand on his arm, looking at him with a special look that said, '*It's going to be okay.*'

He nodded, and she said to them, "Kids, we are really proud of you. Really proud. We know you're going to be okay because you're both smart and resourceful. You've grown up on a farm and know how to work hard and be safe. But please, for goodness' sake, work TOGETHER! And don't fight the whole time! Or I'm worried Seamus here will throw you both out of the boat!"

They all laughed, the tension easing out of the air. Tori and Hudson both promised to be extra good, to be nice to each other, to write in the book, and all the other things they knew they should say. Then both of them went over to their parents and gave them a long hug.

Things had seemed pretty scary the last few days, but now they had a plan. And having a plan felt better than not having anything at all.

Each of them went upstairs to their rooms to get their bags together.

Seamus, who seemed to have taken a liking to Hudson, went with him, and Malcolm joined Tori.

* * *

Tori and Malcolm chatted like the oldest friends as she pulled out her backpack and filled it with things for the trip. Each of them was tripping over each other's words as they rushed to catch up on each other's lives. She wanted to hear how his family was and the forest he lived in, and he was interested in her friends, school, and the farm.

"The journal has been great to keep in touch," Tori smiled, putting her journal in the bag and then pulling clothes from her dresser, "but it just isn't the same as seeing you, Malcolm. It is so great!" She stopped to give him yet another big hug.

"I agree, Tori, our friendship is such a treasure," Malcolm grinned as he helped fold things and arrange them in her pack. "Oh Tori!" he exclaimed, "don't forget that magic stone we gave you from the Land of Fire!"

"Oh, that's right!" Tori went to her secret compartment and removed a small stone from the drawer. As she held it, it immediately warmed up her hand and lower arm. It had been a gift from the King of the Gallywomps as a thank you for healing his skin disease. It warmed whoever held it. "That should be handy where we're going."

Tori was dressed in shorts and a tank top. It was hot and humid outside. But if they were going up to the North Pole, she might need that magic stone for some extra warmth.

"I guess I should be packing warmer clothes, huh?" she asked Malcolm, going to her closet to get her winter coat.

"Yes indeed!" Malcolm agreed. "Even in summer, it will be freezing in the Arctic. Speaking of, I'd better go make sure Seamus has told Hudson that, too."

He hopped off the bed and wandered over to Hudson's room. Tori couldn't help but grin at seeing a tiny gnome walking around in her room. With his cute red hat and long beard, he was everything she'd ever imagined about a gnome, but in real life.

Malcolm found Seamus and Hudson looking through fossils and feather collections. "Come on, you two," he chided, "time's a wasting. Best make sure that Master Hudson has lots of warm clothes."

"Don't worry about me, Malcolm!" Hudson exclaimed. "I always run hot. I'm like a little furnace, my mom says!" But he still pulled out pants, a hockey jersey, and a sweatshirt and stuffed them all into his backpack.

"Wonderful, wonderful," Malcolm replied. "Well, I'll leave you to it and go downstairs to see if your parents can help restore the food provisions." Gnomes always enjoyed knowing where their next meal was coming from.

It was mid-afternoon by the time they had everything ready to go, but Seamus was insistent they should still get started that day. "Won't it get dark?" Hudson asked. "Should we wait until tomorrow?"

"Not to worry, laddie, the underground rivers don't have morning or night. They are always lit with the soft glow of the crystal ceilings. It will be as bright as the night on a full moon. Plenty bright enough once your eyes get used to the dark."

"But we should take our headlamps! Just in case!" He ran off to get two lamps for them.

Once they were ready and had everything packed away, they realized it was time to say goodbye to their parents. Unlike Tori's last adventure, where she didn't tell them the truth about where she was, she felt much better about them knowing. But in some ways, she was even more nervous because of everything that had happened this week. The earthquakes, tornadoes, and the neighbor who had died, things felt a lot more real and a lot scarier.

She gulped down her fear and said out loud, more to herself than anyone, "Don't worry, Mom, we are going to find Santa's elves. How scary can that be?'

Her mom pulled her into a hug, sensing fear in her daughter. Then she pulled Hudson in, too. "You're both going to be fine. I'm sure of it. But don't forget to write each day, okay?" Hudson nodded, holding her tight." And say hi to Santa if you meet him!" she grinned, not quite believing she'd just said that.

Hudson and Tori gathered up their bags, and the gnomes packed up sandwiches and snacks. Their Dad gave them lots of last-minute advice on what they should or shouldn't do. But soon enough, they had all made their way outside and over to a great walnut tree by the meadow. At the base of the tree was a large hole.

Hudson looked at the hole. "Where did that come from? I know this tree better than anyone, and that was never there before."

Seamus and Malcolm both grinned, "Not a thing gets by you, does it, my friend. We gnomes have a bit of magic, you know. A tiny illusion charm is all that is needed to hide our entrances to the underground rivers. It wouldn't do to have young pups like you dropping into the caves. Wouldn't do at all. Well, say your goodbyes, and we will see you down at the bottom."

With that, Malcolm bowed in gratitude to Hudson's mom and dad, red hat bobbing, and hopped down the hole, disappearing from sight. Seamus did the same, his blue hat almost touching the ground in a bow of respect. As he followed Malcolm down the hole at the base of the walnut tree, Tori went over to the hole.

"Hudson," she explained, "Don't worry, it's like a really fun slide. You just jump in, and then you land at the bottom on the shore of the underground river. You go first. I'll be right behind you."

Hudson went over and peered into the black hole, feeling a bit nervous. But Tori had done this before, and he trusted her.

He went over to his parents one last time to tell them he loved them and then returned to the hole. He stood at the edge, looked down, and looked up again at his parents. He took a deep breath and grinned, eyes wide. "See ya!" he called out and boldly jumped into the hole.

It was pitch black, but it felt just like one of those covered slides at the park. It was soft and smooth, and he laughed as he whizzed down and down the hole. After a minute or two of sliding, he plunked down onto what felt like soft sand. It was still dark, but he heard the gnomes calling his name. "Hudson? Is that you, lad?"

"Ooh, that was fun! Let's do it again!" he called back to them.

He stood up just as he heard Tori land on the ground beside him.

"Hey, does anyone have a flashlight?" she asked, her eyes not yet adjusted. Hudson pulled out the headlamps, turning his on and giving her the other one.

"Thanks!" she said. They could now see the gnomes standing next to Seamus' boat and walked over to join them.

"Just as I remembered it!" she said, "though it looks a little smaller than last time." The old, but well-maintained wooden boat was quite spacious by gnome standards, but Tori had grown half a foot since last year, and the middle seats seemed a bit small.

Seamus looked up at her, "Oy, it's not smaller, you've just gotten bigger. But we'll still fit, not to worry."

They piled into the boat, with Seamus at the back by the rudder and Malcolm up front. Seamus began to explain to Hudson about the rivers.

"Now, lad, these underground rivers connect all over the world. They run fast and are the greatest way to travel somewhere quickly. The water flows on its own, so all that needs doing is sharp eyes and good steering. Malcolm's the eyes, and I keep to the steering. If you want to help him, too, we can turn that lamp off, and soon you'll see there's enough light to see."

Hudson turned off his light, looking around in the dim tunnel as he settled into his wooden seat.

"Tori," Seamus looked over to her as she also switched off her light. "You may remember these rivers were quite relaxing. Well, not since the quakes. So many rocks fell, blocking the water, that the channels that are still open are faster than ever. It's going to take all of us staying on our toes to make sure we avoid rocks. Have you ever gone rafting on rapids?"

"No," she said, a little concerned. "Is it dangerous?"

"Not a bit," he replied, "just keep sharp and follow my lead. We may have to go from one side of the boat to the other, or use these oars to turn." He gave each of them a short oar. "The North Passage is one of the most exciting rivers I navigate. But now, well, it's gotten a bit wild." He laughed a little madly, "But who doesn't like a bit of adventure?"

The kids grimaced, equal parts excitement and fear, and gripped their oars tightly as Seamus pushed the boat off into the river.

* * *

At first, the stream they were in was smooth and gentle. Tori wondered if Seamus had been exaggerating, but as they left that tunnel and joined a bigger one, things started to pick up quickly. The tunnel was about as wide as a road and almost as tall. The ceiling was full of softly glowing crystals that lit the passage like a bright moonlit night. She could see in that light that there were cracks in the ceiling that hadn't been there when she last traveled on these rivers.

"Are these the cracks you mentioned? Where the rocks have fallen?" she asked.

"Ay, but you'll see they get worse as we keep going," Seamus explained. "But they're a good clue. Wherever you see cracks, keep an eye out for boulders in the river. We either need to steer to avoid them or ride through the rapids they make. It's like a raging river in the mountains, full of twists and turns. We just take one section at a time, figuring out what to do with what we find." He paused and pointed up to Malcolm at the bow of the boat. "Malcolm will keep an eye out, too. He knows what to look for."

The river started to move swiftly as water rushed in from the side tunnels. Hudson pointed out cracks along the ceiling, and Malcolm would shout back to Seamus about boulders up ahead. The water would swirl and eddy as it moved around the boulders, and the boat ride got quite bumpy.

Seamus was steering from the stern to avoid the boulders, but soon the river turned into raging rapids, and they were moving too fast for just his steering. He told the kids to get their oars ready.

Malcolm called back to Seamus, "Boulder to the left, hard to the right!"

Seamus adjusted the rudder. "Both of you, oars in on the right and row hard!" Tori and Hudson put all their muscles into the rowing and avoided a massive boulder. As soon as they got through that rapid, suddenly Malcolm called back, "Hard to the left now!"

They threw the oars in and pulled the boat to the left, narrowly avoiding a giant rock that had fallen into the middle of the river.

Then they heard Malcolm cry out, "Whirlpool!! Pull back!"

"Row backward, kids. Give it all you've got!" Seamus called to them as he pushed the rudder. Their backward motion flipped them around, and they narrowly edged past an angry whirlpool that had been trying to pull them in. "Ay! That was it!"

Back and forth, Tori and Hudson used their oars and all their strength to go through rapids and around boulders. Water would fly up and over the bow, splashing their faces. Sometimes the boulders would be so close they had to pull the oars in entirely, barely scraping through the passage. Forwards, backwards, left, right, it was all happening so fast. They just went on instinct.

Finally, the river calmed down. There were no cracks in the ceilings, and the water flowed smoothly.

"Wow," Hudson exhaled. "That was intense!"

Seamus beamed, "You two did amazing. Absolutely amazing! Well done! So, what do you think of the North Passage?"

Tori looked around, also exhaling as the danger had passed. "I love it!"

They took advantage of this short, quiet section to pass around sandwiches. "We have to keep our strength up," Seamus said unapologetically as he devoured a cheese sandwich.

"I agree," Malcolm said, eating his sandwich and an apple. "But eat quickly, children. We have more rapids to get through before we can call it a night."

The kids were still running high on excitement and adrenaline. They didn't feel hungry, but they ate their sandwiches and had a quick drink from their water bottles. They'd barely finished when they hit another set of rapids. "Here we go again!" Malcolm called back.

"To the left," he shouted. They just made it around a huge boulder.

"Now, forward on," Seamus called out as Tori and Hudson put their oars in to row forward. "Ay, straight through!" Malcolm agreed, pointing to boulders on both sides of them.

The four of them worked in unison, the boat weaving through each twist and turn the river threw at them.

As they got past another whirlpool, Tori and Hudson grinned at each other, hair and clothes soaked. Seamus looked at them proudly from the back of the boat. "The North Passage gives us two choices. To come together, or be torn apart. Glad everyone's working together so well.

Well done, Team!" Malcolm looked back and gave them a thumbs up. "Looks clear for a bit ahead. Take a breath."

They traveled quickly and smoothly for several minutes before Seamus announced, "Okay, team, up ahead a section of the tunnel's caved in. We need to secure all the loose items. The tunnel floor's cracked, and let's just say we have a big drop ahead."

Hudson's eyes widened.

"Not to worry, laddie. We'll take it straight on and no one will fall out. Just follow my directions."

They could see boulders to the left, right, and center, and the speed was picking up. "Now here's what we need to do. First, we go left around the big rock in the center. Then, hard right back to avoid the one on the left. Then pull back to center us out and avoid the one on the right. Got it?"

Hudson, feeling courageous, yelled, "We got it, Captain Douglas! Let's go!"

They rushed into the rapids, pulling hard on the oars. Left, right, then back to center. They could see the water dropping in front of them into a waterfall. "Hold on!" Malcolm called back, grabbing onto the boat's side.

And over the edge they went. A moment in the air that seemed to stretch on for a lifetime, and then a huge smack as the boat dropped back into the river. The river splashed up and soaked their things, but they were safe and sound.

"Well then, Malcolm," Seamus called up to the front of the boat. "I think we've earned a bit of a rest!"

"Indeed, we have!" Malcolm agreed. They came around a bend in the river and saw it had widened out. There was a bit of beach to the side, and Seamus steered the boat over.

As they got out of the boat, they saw a campfire ring and a stack of neatly piled wood. It was not the first time someone had the same idea to stop at this beach.

"Ah, perfect, Seamus," Malcolm grinned as he walked over to the firewood. "Always prepared, I see."

"Well, of course, my friend, of course!" He chuckled. "Any good boat captain knows that all passengers need to stop for tea time."

"Tea time?" Hudson looked at Tori. Tori laughed, "Yeah, the gnomes love their tea. And cake. And picnic lunches." Just as she said that, she saw Seamus pulling a basket out of the back of the boat and bringing it over to Malcolm, who was starting a fire in the stone fire ring.

Before long, they were all sitting around a roaring fire, with a pot of tea brewed, and dinner laid out on a cozy checkered cloth.

The heat from the fire helped dry out their soaked clothes, and they finished the dried fruits, nuts, and cheese that the gnomes had laid out. They even had little mini cakes with peach jam in the center. "Where did you get those?" Hudson asked. "They're delicious!"

Malcolm grinned and said, "Little-known fact, but Seamus is an excellent baker!" Tori and Hudson looked surprised, having learned something new about their river captain.

"Aww, just a wee hobby," Seamus mumbled shyly, smiling.

As Tori finished her cake, she realized how tired she was. "Are we going to keep going tonight in these rapids?" she asked, yawning. She'd lost sense of time in the underground tunnels, but remembered they'd set out late in the afternoon.

Seamus looked at them knowingly, "No lassie, I think we all need a bit of rest before we tackle the rest of the North Passage. We don't want anyone falling out of the boat, and the more tired we get, the more dangerous it can be. We should have a good night's sleep here on this beach. It is one of the safest spots we could pull off, and we won't be disturbed."

"Sounds good!' Hudson agreed. "I'm exhausted. Where are the beds?" He looked around at the sandy beach.

"Come with me," Seamus said, standing up, and Hudson followed him over to a dry spot on the beach. Bedrolls and wool blankets had been stored in a neat pile next to the firewood. As Hudson helped carry the beds over, Seamus said kindly to him, "I must say you're taking to all this adventure!"

Hudson smiled and shrugged. "Yeah, it's not too scary so far. It's been fun!" He helped Seamus lay out all the beds for everyone, forming a circle around the warm fire. Everyone settled into bed and wished each other goodnight.

Within minutes of heads hitting the pillows, the soft sound of gnome snores began to fill the air.

* * *

Hudson could hear Tori's breathing and the gnome's gentle snoring, but he tossed and turned, unable to sleep. He kept thinking about his parents, his neighbors, and his friends. He was worried, wondering if they were okay. He imagined a dozen different catastrophes, each one worse than the last. But his body was so tired from the day, and he begged his mind to be quiet.

He pulled Tori's magic journal out of her bag to see if his mom had written. There was a short message.

We love you so much. Be safe. Love, Mom and Dad

He got out a pen and wrote:

Hi Mom, We went on crazy rapids today but we're ok. Miss u. Love, Hudson

69

He put the book away, at least knowing they were okay for now. Finally, exhausted, he fell into a restless sleep. But his dreams carried on his worries.

A nightmare woke him. Muffling a scream, he bolted upright. He looked around, expecting to see his bedroom at home, but realized he was in a strange underground tunnel.

Seamus, woken by Hudson's scream, came over. He'd taken a kindness to Hudson during their day together. They both shared adventure in their bones.

"Aww laddie," he said softly, his gray-blue eyes crinkling, "Not to worry, ol' Seamus is here with you." Seamus sat down and put his weather-worn hand on Hudson's head. "Go ahead and sleep now. I'll stay by your side. Everything's going to be okay." Hudson lay back down. Seamus patted his head of curly blonde hair, soothing him with a soft but strong presence. Hudson liked Seamus, too. He appreciated his directness and boldness. Hudson figured that if Seamus said things were going to be okay, he could trust him. He had sailed these rivers before and knew where the dangers were. Hudson allowed himself to be comforted by the wizened old gnome and eventually fell back to sleep.

Though there was no morning or night in the underground world of rivers and caves, their internal clocks called them to wake. Malcolm, who always seemed to be up early, was the first to rise. He rebuilt the fire and put the kettle on to make some tea. As the water was boiling, Hudson and Seamus woke up. Tori was the slowest to move. It seemed the older she got, the more she loved sleeping. She yawned and stretched, uncurling herself from her blankets.

Tori had forgotten to put her curly hair in a braid the night before, so it frizzed out in every direction. She brushed it down and pulled it back as she went over to the river to wash the sleep off her face. Hudson was helping Malcolm cook up oatmeal, or porridge as Malcolm called it, and Tori came over to help, too.

As they all sat down to breakfast, Malcolm remarked, "You know, I don't think the two of you fought once yesterday. Tori, I thought you said you didn't get along with your little brother."

"I don't!" she defended quickly. "But," she reflected, "I guess sometimes we come together when it's important. And I suppose this is pretty important."

"Well said," Seamus applauded. "This is more important than any of our differences. I don't think we told you all that we saw on the way here. Maybe we shouldn't actually. But things are bad. Pretty bad."

Tori had heard on the radio that there was a lot of destruction from the earthquakes and the storms, but she hadn't seen it herself. She'd been on the farm, where there hadn't been too much damage. She knew her dad had gone around to help others and didn't want to talk about what he saw.

"It's okay if you want to tell us," she said to Seamus. "We can handle it. You don't need to keep things from us."

Seamus dropped his eyes and sighed. "Oh no, lassie, it's not that I'm trying to protect you. I know you are both strong and brave." He gave them a little wink. "I just don't see the point in going over and over again all the bad things that have happened. I'm a bit of an action guy, if you noticed. I want to jump into how to make things better!" He jumped up, putting his porridge bowl down. "And that's what we shall do! Alright then, who's ready to get on the river and back to some more adventure! Let's find these Weavers and the answers to all this madness!"

Hudson and Tori jumped up, too, and Malcolm grinned so wide his red hat bobbed a bit. "Hear, hear, Seamus! Who knows what tomorrow brings, but let's make the best of today!"

As they started to clean up breakfast and repack their bags, Hudson asked, "How many more days will we be on the river to get to the North Pole?"

Seamus replied enthusiastically, "Days? No, lad, we're more than halfway there!"

Tori was shocked by his response. "How is that possible? That's even faster than it took us to get to Scotland last year!"

"Ay," Seamus said. "Usually, the North Passage takes three days from where you two live, but the water is flowing so fast now that the time has been cut in half. We're almost past New York and into Canada!"

Hudson wasn't sure of his geography, but he'd gone to New York once with his dad, and it was more than a few hours from his house. "Wow! That is fast! Are we going to have lots of rapids again today? And what happens when we get closer to the North Pole? Is it going to get colder? Will there be ice in the river?"

"Ah, good question about the ice. There will be ice at the North Pole, but not down here in the rivers. We are so far below the surface of the Earth that the temperature stays constant. Unless you go near a volcano! Then it gets a bit warmer. Did Tori tell you about us going to Iceland? It was positively sweltering there! Hot enough to make my beard sweat!"

Hudson laughed, imagining a gnome with a sweaty beard.

"But as for the rapids, I'm not sure, lad. I've only been this far north recently. Malcolm and I came over from Scotland to collect you two, and this is the passage we traveled down. There's a junction just ahead that takes us North or East toward Scotland. We'll go North, a straight shot up to the Pole. Let's ask Malcolm what he thinks about the rapids. He's got a map with all the fault lines in the world. That's where the earthquakes were, so it may tell us if we are in for more tunnel collapses or smooth sailing."

Malcolm, who had been over in the corner stacking the bedrolls and blankets, returned to the group. "Malcolm," Hudson asked, "Seamus said you had a map that showed if there could be more tunnel collapses ahead. Could we see it?"

"Ah, yes!" Malcolm put his hand into the pocket of his coat and pulled out a large map of the world. It showed the land above in faint gray and all the underground rivers in dark blue. Overlaid on top of the rivers were red dashed lines dividing the land masses. "These are the fault lines," he pointed to the red lines. "And this is the river we're on. You can see that we went through two already." He pointed to two lines that crossed over the blue river on the map. "And this is where we're going. This River. See, it says 'North Passage.' Now look at these red lines. They run parallel to us, alongside the river. So, it should be pretty clear. Right up to this point."

He pointed to a thick black line. "This isn't a fault line. It's more of a," he paused, looking for the right word, "barrier. A magical barrier that keeps folks from going into the Land of the Elves."

"What will we need to go through it?" Tori asked, looking at the map. In her last adventure, they had to pay a toll to pass through the land of the Gallywomps. She wondered if some kind of payment was needed, but she hadn't brought any money with her.

"Well, you don't need anything to get through it, but it will still be a bit tricky to find our way," Malcolm explained. "It is the Veil of Illusion, a mist that tries to keep us from getting to the Land of the Elves. You have to want to get through it, to really believe in your purpose; otherwise, you get lost in it. Tori, kind of like when you had to find your magic to save the Phoenix. You had to believe that you could do it."

"Well, of course we believe," Hudson exclaimed. "That's why we're here, isn't it?"

"Well said," Malcolm replied. He folded the map and put it back in his pocket. "That is why we are here! So, let's head off to the North

Pole, my friends! What do you say, Captain Douglas? Are we ready to go?"

"Ay! Ready and waiting!" Seamus exclaimed. "The North Passage calls!" They gathered their bags and piled back into the boat to meet their next day of adventure on the river.

* * *

Eight

The Veil of Illusion

The children were excited to have a smooth day after the rapids of yesterday. Since Malcolm's map had shown no fault lines, Seamus had them stow their oars.

Things were easygoing for once. There were no cracks in the ceiling and no rocks to avoid. The water was swift but smooth. Hudson and Tori could finally relax and enjoy the experience of traveling in an underground river surrounded by beautiful glowing crystals.

After a couple hours Malcolm stepped away from his lookout at the front to have a snack with the kids. He'd just passed around dried fruits and nuts when the boat started to bounce.

Choppy waves came up out of nowhere. They'd been through plenty of rapids yesterday, but not waves like this. They were like waves in the ocean, not a river.

Hudson jumped up and looked to the bow. "Seamus!' he called back. "What's happening?"

"I'm not sure," Seamus answered, taking a stiff hold of the rudder. "I can't see anything ahead. Can you?"

Hudson couldn't see any fallen rocks or cracks in the ceiling that would indicate the earthquakes had struck here. Yet, the waves increased in height and frequency. The boat went up and crashed down over the crest of each wave. The children were jolted from their seats, spilling the snacks Malcolm had served.

"Brace yourselves!" Seamus called out and secured a rope around his waist that had been tied to the boat.

The waves grew in intensity, rocking the wooden boat like a play toy in a stormy sea. Tori saw some rope coiled at her feet. She quickly made a knot she'd learned at camp and secured one end of the rope to the seat of the boat. She wrapped the other end in a loop around her little brother. "I won't lose you off the side of the boat!" she exclaimed. "Mom would kill me!" She then wrapped a loop around her own waist.

They couldn't figure out what was causing these waves, but they were as bad as any rapids. The boat galloped along like a wild mustang trying to throw its rider. Crashing down after each wave, a loose blanket and a water bottle flew out of the boat and into the river. Hudson's oar almost went over, but he grabbed it just in time.

"What on earth is causing these waves?" Malcolm wondered, trying to hold himself and all the supplies down in the boat.

And then Hudson saw it. He had turned to look back at Seamus, and saw it coming at them through the tunnel. His jaw dropped. Speechless, he pointed behind the boat.

"What is it?" Tori asked, turning around.

"Seamus!" she screamed."Look out!"

A wall of water was rushing towards them. It filled the tunnel, all the way to the ceiling, like a giant tsunami. The other waves had just been the preamble. Here was the main event.

"Oh sh…" Malcolm stopped himself before he said something he shouldn't.

"Hold onto each other and hold your breath," Seamus yelled, putting one hand on the boat and taking hold of Hudson with the other.

The wave washed over them, and suddenly they were all underwater. Tori held her breath, trying not to panic. The boat was still moving forward, but it was now inside the wave. The water carried the boat almost to the top of the tunnel. The ceiling was inches from her head.

Her lungs began to hurt from holding her breath. She looked at Hudson and the gnomes, weightless in the water. They began to float up out of their seats, but the rope kept them inside the boat. Hudson's eyes started to bulge, struggling to hold his breath any longer. Malcolm's hat was floating up off his head, and he fought to grab it and still hold onto his seat. Most of their supplies were drifting out of the boat. There was nothing they could do but hold on and hope the wave passed before they ran out of air.

Seconds crawled by while they held their breath. And then, as quickly as it came, the wave washed over them. The boat dropped out of the water and back into gravity. It slid backwards as it fell from the top of the wave back down into the river, and landed with a thump.

Everyone exhaled, Malcolm coughing water out of his mouth. Tori patted him on the back to help clear his lungs. They were soaking wet, but remarkably alive.

"What was that?" Hudson stuttered, shaken from the experience.

Seamus looked around, taking an assessment of his boat. "Honestly, son, I have no idea. In all my years, I've not seen anything like that. It was like a tidal wave."

Tori loosened the rope she'd put around herself and her brother. "It must have been from the earthquakes. That's what causes them in the ocean. We would have drowned if it had gone on much longer."

Malcolm nodded, still coughing a bit. "We could have. I don't think I could have held my breath for another second."

Seamus steered the boat off to a side channel so they could stop and put the boat and themselves back together. They'd lost quite a few supplies, but miraculously, the children's backpacks had stayed wedged under their seats. Malcolm had sat on the bag that contained their food for the day. "Priorities," he said sheepishly. Hudson had grabbed both oars, and the boat hadn't been damaged. It felt like they lucked out.

Tori laughed a bit, now that the danger was over. "Well, I guess this gives a whole new meaning to going with the flow."

Hudson groaned at the joke as he squeezed water from his shirt. "So, Malcolm, does your map have any more of those in store?"

"I sure hope not," Malcolm shook his head. "Let's keep that to once in a lifetime. Are you both okay to keep going? I know you didn't sign up for possible drownings on this adventure."

The face of resilience, both kids nodded.

"Sure, why not?" Hudson said, shrugging his shoulders. "We've come this far! I think the four of us can handle anything this river throws at us!"

"I like that attitude!" Seamus brightened up, hearing Hudson's enthusiasm. "I knew you had an adventurous heart the moment I met you, wee man. And there's no use sitting around worrying about what comes next. Better to just go out and face it head on."

They all agreed. Determined to keep going, they put the boat back in order, secured the few provisions they had left, and headed back out into the river.

* * *

As they returned to the North Passage, they didn't run into any more waves, but the speed picked up dramatically. Seamus wondered if it was the extra volume of water from the wave. Whatever it was, they were positively flying down the river. It was all he could do to steer them straight through the tunnel.

The tunnel ceiling was filled with quartz crystals that glowed with a supernatural light. They were like thousands of stars on a clear night. With all that starlight reflecting and refracting in the crystals, it created a soft glow. But that was when one was traveling at a nice, slow speed.

When the boat was going faster than a car speeding down a highway, the refracting lights looked like they were traveling through a time warp tunnel. Lights flashed by faster than their eyes could track, making the ceiling look like a swirly blur.

But Captain Douglas knew his boat, and he expertly guided them through the river's twists and turns. Hours passed without a break in the fast-moving flow. The boat sped along the river like a rocket ship traveling past the stars, with Seamus navigating and Malcolm keeping an eye out for fallen rocks. Tori and Hudson held on to the sides of their seats, awestruck by the speed at which the boat was flying along the tunnel.

Eventually, Malcolm looked back at Seamus and could see the strain on his stoic face. "Think we need to pull off for a break, friend?" He was concerned that this speed and maneuvering were too much even for his travel-hardy companion.

"Ay," Seamus grimaced. "That would be nice indeed, but I'm afraid we have a bit to go before we could even stop. The water's higher than I've ever seen it, and all the normal pull-offs are flooded over. We'll have to carry on for a bit longer."

Tori and Hudson also looked at Seamus, realizing the toll this was taking on him. They hadn't noticed just how much he was doing behind them, steering the boat back and forth with the rudder. "Can we help, Captain?" Tori asked. "Just for a bit? We can use our oars to help steer."

"Oh, thank you, Tori," he smiled. "I appreciate the offer. I should be alright for a wee bit longer, but if I do get tired, I'll be sure to have you put your oars in."

They carried on for another hour or so and noticed the water was gradually slowing down. The river was also getting wider, so there was more room for the water to flow. Seamus visibly relaxed as the waters calmed. Tori exhaled loudly and realized the tension she'd been holding as they had been barreling down the river. Malcolm passed sandwiches and snacks around to everyone. They drank from their water bottles and took in the scenery now that they were going slow enough to see. It felt like the worst of the North Passage was behind them.

As Hudson finished his sandwich, he noticed a light mist beginning to form just above the river surface. It moved and shifted as they passed by. In some areas, it was barely there. In others, it was denser, almost opaque. He pointed to the mist as it began to swirl close to the boat. "What's that? It doesn't look like normal fog. It looks like it's moving!"

Hudson and Tori both peered into the mist swirling around them. It thickened in spots, creating shapes. At first, they formed spheres and spirals. Then they began to form objects. "Is that a chair?" Tori asked, pointing to the right side of the boat.

"And look, that looks like a tree!" Hudson called out as he pointed to the left.

"Ay," Seamus called out. "The mists form the Veil of Illusion. They will turn into just about anything you can imagine." He paused, a concerned look on his face. "And some things you can't. Steady on through the veil, my friends. No matter what you see, remember our purpose here."

Malcolm added, "Tori and Hudson, the mists are meant to distract us, so that we stop our journey. Many have gotten lost in here for months and years. Lost in their dreams, forgetting reality. Don't lose sight of our mission."

Hudson peered over the stern. The mists were thickening and taking on more fantastic shapes. They began to turn into a house with a front porch. It looked just like his house. The mists began to form trees, and then people. It was his family and the dogs. They had smiles on their faces, and it looked like they were laughing. The mists even began to form his chicken house, perfect and intact.

He began to wonder what they were doing on this boat in an underground river. The adventure through the rapids had been fun, but maybe it was time to go back home. He missed his dogs and patrolling the farm with them. He missed his bedroom and all his stuff. The mists responded to his thoughts. They changed shape and turned into his bedroom. He saw a perfect image of his bed with lots of pillows, his fossil collection, his rainbow lamp, and a stack of books. He could almost see the book with his hockey collectible cards on top.

"What was our purpose again?" he asked dreamily, looking at the scene. He felt if he could reach just a bit farther, he'd be able to pick up the book. He got up from the wooden seat, extending his arm out into the water. The vision pulled back a bit. He reached out a little further. It was so close, the safety and security of home. He lifted one foot up and over the hull.

"Hang on there, laddie." Seamus jumped from his spot and pulled Hudson back in. Without realizing it, Hudson had almost walked right off the boat and into the river!

Hudson looked dazed, as if he was still in a dream. Seamus held onto him as he guided him back to his seat.

Meanwhile, Tori was having her own daydream. The mists had solidified into an ice-skating rink on her side of the boat. She could see herself and her friends out figure skating. Looping around, they moved from one foot to the other, and then twirled together perfectly at the same time. She could almost hear their laughter. The scene became so real that she could see the twinkle in her friend Julie's eyes as she skated closer to her. It was almost like she was reaching out for a hug. Tori reached back, extending her arms out over the boat.

"Not so fast!" Seamus quickly grabbed Tori, pulling her back into the boat.

"We need to put some seat belts on you two!" Malcolm called out in alarm. He had been seeing his own misty daydreams, his home far away in Scotland, filled with family laughing and cooking. But he knew it was a dream. He hadn't told the children, but the tree he lived in had come crashing down in the earthquake. His home had been destroyed, as had many of his neighbors' homes. The misty vision looked lovely, but he knew it wasn't real.

The children shook their heads, clearing the daydreams from their eyes. But the mists weren't done with them. It was almost as if it knew they couldn't be distracted with beautiful visions of happy scenes. So, the mist started to take on a different tone.

Hudson's happy scene of his room began to dissolve. It turned into the front yard they'd left yesterday, with the trees fallen and the chicken coop destroyed. His parents were outside working in the yard, fixing the chicken coop. The image was a perfect vision of their home, down to the bikes sitting on the front porch. He could even see his mom's lips moving, almost hear her talking.

Then the mists began to form clouds in the distance, creating a darkening sky. A tornado formed in the clouds. It began to swirl menacingly at the edge of the scene, and it grew more solid as it moved towards his house. His parents didn't see it, but it was coming straight for them.

"Mom! Dad! Look out!" he yelled, reaching out towards the illusion, trying to save them. It was so real, it looked like a portal to what was happening at home right now. "Tori!" he grabbed his sister's arm, pointing to the mist. "Mom and Dad! Another tornado is coming!"

He turned back to Seamus, "We have to turn around! We have to save them!"

But Seamus didn't answer. He was looking over the edge of the boat. The mists had created his own terror. "No!" he called out, lost in the mists. "Not them. Please spare them! They didna' do anything."

Tori could feel panic rising inside her. Everything darkened around her except for the image in front of Hudson. The tornado coming right for their house. "It's not real, Hudson!" she shook him. "It's not real!"

She closed her eyes, refusing to look. She reached out to hold her brother's hand. She kept saying over and over again. "It's not real. It's not real." She squeezed his trembling hand. "Say it with me, Hudson. It's not real. It's not real. It's just an illusion."

Fear in his voice, he joined her. "You're not real. You're just an illusion. Go away."

He wanted to close his eyes, but he couldn't. The tornado ripped through their house, sending wood flying everywhere. Everything that had been saved from the first round of tornadoes and earthquakes was getting sucked up into the swirling wind. His parents ran, but they couldn't run fast enough. "You're not real," he whispered in horror, as the mist showed his parents getting sucked up into the tornado. "You're not real." Tears started to flow down his cheeks. His dogs ran fast, but the tornado chased them down. "You're just an illusion. Go away." His whole body trembled, as he watched his dog Goose get swept up into the tornado.

Then he heard a voice speaking to them from a distance. It was Malcolm's voice, but it felt like miles away.

"Tori. Hudson. Remember why we are here." They stared at the mist, unable to look at Malcolm, but he'd pulled them back just a bit from their horror. "Why we're here?" Tori asked, in a daze. "I can't remember. It all seems so bleak. Everything's gone. Our family, our Home. Everything. Gone."

Malcolm said loudly and solemnly, "Then let me remind you of why we are here. Or I should say, why YOU are here." He pulled the scroll out of his pocket and unfurled it. "Let me read the prophecy to you again. The one that the Weavers wrote all those years ago."

"And a time of great stress and strain in humanity will come, and the world will also feel that strain. The Earth will crack and buckle, and great cities will fall. Storms will sweep the seas and the forests, washing away the old ways of greed and power. Governments will crumble, and the old will look to the young to lead them into the future. From the ashes of the Phoenix, a new epoch will be born. A time of peace and harmony. A time of love and light. And the young will lead the way."

As Malcolm read the words out loud, they echoed on the walls of the tunnel, and then there was silence. The mists began to dissolve around them. The scene of the home and the tornado disappeared. They could see the walls of the cave and the river beside them. Tori looked at Hudson, his cheeks wet with tears. She wiped her own eyes. "Remember, it wasn't real." She hugged him tightly. "It was just an illusion." They looked back at Seamus, who was coming out of a daze. He looked as shaken as they were, and she wondered what he'd seen.

"Thank you, my friend," Seamus called up to Malcolm. "I don't know what would have happened if you hadn't stepped in there. It felt so real." his voice trailed off as he looked around.

The mists began to form again around them. At first, Tori felt fear rise in her gut, but then she saw they were coming together differently. Instead of creating shapes and images, the mist was creating a tunnel.

It was a tunnel of fog within the tunnel. It thickened so much that they couldn't see the rock walls or the crystal ceiling above. The only thing they could see was a narrow opening in front of them. It was an arch, just as tall and wide as the boat.

Seamus steered the boat toward the arch, responding to the mist's direction.

"It seems the Veil liked that prophecy, Malcolm," he said, as they glided forward through this tight tunnel of cloud.

"Ay," Malcolm replied thoughtfully. "It does indeed. It's almost as if…."

Hudson interrupted. "The mists recognized the words. Like they knew why we were here, even when we forgot."

"Indeed," Malcolm nodded. "Yes, indeed. Captain, let us follow where this tunnel takes us. I think it may be showing us the way, instead of trying to distract us."

"Agreed, Master Malcolm. I suppose now is the time for a bit of trust and faith."

The four of them moved smoothly and quietly down the river, into the tunnel of mist.

Tori and Hudson sat closer together, nervous in the deep fog. Malcolm lit a lantern, as the mist had blocked out all the light from the ceiling. Seamus steered cautiously. They couldn't see if there were any rocks to their sides, so he kept tight within the archway. All they could see was the narrow path before them and the light at the front of the boat. Everything else was gray, misty darkness.

Tori thought she could see faces in the mist, but she didn't want to look too closely and be distracted again. Instead, she looked straight ahead, focusing on Malcolm's light and the path ahead of them in the river.

They turned a bend in the river, and the fog shifted. It began to move to the left while the river was turning to the right.

"Seamus," Malcolm called back. "Follow the fog. We have to trust it is taking us where we need to go."

Seamus didn't have much choice. The fog was a thick, impenetrable wall everywhere except for the path ahead. He steered the boat to the left, hoping they wouldn't crash into the tunnel wall. They could see the rock ahead as the boat drew closer. The fog narrowed. They were heading right towards the wall.

"Seamus!" Hudson called out. "Watch out! We're going to hit that wall!"

Hudson grabbed Tori's hand, terrified. The fog thickened all around them, and the wall grew closer.

"Seamus!" Tori screamed. "Stop!"

Malcolm replied calmly, almost serenely, "Not everything is as it seems, my friends. You are in a magic place. Keep the faith."

Their senses were screaming to stop. Turn back. But Malcolm stood at the front of the boat, stoically facing the impending collision. Ten feet, five feet, two feet. Tori and Hudson braced for impact.

Hudson ducked his head down and closed his eyes. Then, just as the impact should have happened, the air shifted.

He looked up. They were alive! The boat was still intact and moving through the water. The fog was gone, and the wall of rock was beyond them.

"What the…" Hudson looked around, struggling to make sense of the situation.

Seamus grinned, "Well, thank ye kindly, Master Mist. We'd surely not have found this entrance without ye."

Tori was the first to catch on. "Was that a magical entrance? Like a secret door that just looked like a wall?"

"Spot on, Tori," Malcolm smiled, as he also exhaled. "Or at least I certainly hoped it was and that the mists weren't leading us to our doom!"

Now that certain death had been avoided, the children looked around and took in the change of surroundings. The stone walls and crystal ceiling of the underground river had been replaced by a tunnel of ice. The clear ice refracted the light of the lamp like a prism, rainbows dancing on the wall. It was also a lot colder. Tori shivered and pulled out her jacket from her bag.

"It's pretty," Hudson mused. "Look at how the light glows in the ice. It's green and blue but also clear. It's like an ice castle!"

The river began to open up as they went. Other small streams joined with theirs, and then merged into a large river, twice as wide as the one they'd traveled on the day before. Beautiful decorations had been carved into the ice walls of the larger river. Lights had been hung in alcoves along the wall, and they flickered and danced like candle flames in the ice.

But all was not perfect, even in this enchanted place. Large cracks lined the ceiling. Breaks in the ice walls from the earthquakes. Chunks of ice floated around them, mini icebergs that Seamus steered around.

They traveled through a huge archway, shaped and decorated with geometric patterns and symbols. Stars and planets had been carved into the top of the archway, and the sides were decorated with majestic trees, flowers twisting up the trunks. Large lamps lined each side, the light reflecting in the blue-green ice, creating an air of magic and mystery. But one side of the archway had fallen away, and the bottom of the trunk was missing.

As they passed through to the other side of the arch, they came out into a large lake.

Hudson's jaw dropped, amazed at how such a massive lake could exist underground. A large beach extended in front of them, with snow drifting onto the sand. There were several other boats pulled onto the shore, and Seamus began to steer towards an opening in the boats.

"Well, here we are!" Malcolm said as they made their way towards the beach.

"Where is here?" Hudson asked, eyes wide in awe.

"The North Pole, of course!" Seamus exclaimed, grinning.

"Already?" Tori asked. "It feels like we just left our house yesterday!"

Seamus laughed, "We did just leave your house yesterday! But in all my years of traveling the North Passage, I've never moved as fast as we did. That was record time!"

Hudson continued to look around, taking in the beach and the snowy trees beyond. "Yeah, it was fast, wasn't it? It almost felt easy."

Seamus grimaced, arms sore from steering the boat through the rapids. He was also still shaking off the disturbing visions he'd seen in the mists. "I don't know about easy, wee man, but I know what you mean. It feels like someone, or something, was watching out for us a bit. Making sure we got here safely, and in just the right time."

Hudson nodded thoughtfully, "Yeah, maybe you're right. Maybe it was magic." Just as he spoke, the front of the boat hit the beach, jostling the passengers. He grinned as he looked down at the soft sand.

They had arrived at the North Pole.

Nine

This is the North Pole?

Malcolm jumped out of the boat, pulling it up onto the snowy shore. Hudson threw on his tie-dye hoodie and got out to help. Once the boat was secure, Tori and Seamus also disembarked. Shivering in the cold, they took in this curious place that was the North Pole.

Hudson had seen plenty of movies about Santa, the elves, and the North Pole, but none of them looked quite like this. Sure, it was cold, and there was snow, but they were underground. Whoever said Santa and his elves lived underground?

He looked up and could see the ceiling of the cavern extended high above them. It glowed with the natural light of daylight, but he couldn't see anything that looked like a sun. The light moved around in the ceiling, almost like clouds passing by, creating shadows on the ground.

He turned around to look at the archway they had come in. It was one of several openings in a decorated wall of crystal ice. But as he turned back to the shoreline, the cavern went on for what looked like miles. The beach turned into rolling hills of snow and trees. Pine and spruce trees covered with a dusting of snow stood tall at the edge of the beach. At the edge of the trees was a stone path that led to a clearing, and he could see buildings in the distance. Buildings underground!

"This is the North Pole?" he asked. "It's cold enough, but why is it below ground? And where's the Pole?" He had a picture in his head of a red and white striped pole that was supposed to sit right next to Santa's house. "And where are the elves? And Santa?"

"Ah, yes, lots of questions," Malcolm chuckled. "I'll start with the first and see if we can get answers to the rest soon enough." He pointed to the caverns and the ceiling. "Most magical things are underground. And the North Pole is the most magical place there is. If it were on the surface, the planes that fly over the Arctic would have discovered it long ago. It would probably be a tourist attraction with people charging money to visit, and the magic would have been ruined. Oh no, no, all the really deep magic in this world is down here, out of view. It keeps it pure and untainted."

Malcolm looked over to Tori, "Your sister got to visit another great underground city, the Land of Fire, where the Gallywomps live. But it was a bit warmer than here, to be sure!"

Tori nodded, "It sure was. The volcanoes made it nice and toasty. And the sky there was red, not white and pearly like the sky here." She pointed up to the ceiling, noticing how the ice crystals made the clouds look pearlescent.

Malcolm continued his explanation, "As for the Pole itself. That's just a story. The North Pole is an area, not one spot. The actual magnetic pole moves around constantly, so if someone tried to mark it, they'd just have to move it all the time. You can ask the elves, but I think it moves something like 50 miles each year! And as for your question about the elves, well, here they come!"

Hudson and Tori looked towards the path and saw a group of children, gnomes, and what must be elves walking their way. The elves were about the same size as the gnomes. They also had pointy hats like the gnomes, but the similarities ended there.

The elves didn't have long beards; most of them didn't have beards at all. They had pointy ears that stuck out past their hats, and a wide variety of hair colors and styles. Some were tall and slim, and others were short and stout. They wore sweaters with festive Christmas colors—red, green, gold, purple, blue, and white. Some had outrageous patterns on them, others had pictures of reindeer and candy canes. They all had matching black shoes, and Hudson was surprised to see that their shoes really did come to a point!

They were laughing and talking happily with the children as they came towards them.

Hudson noticed the children had a wide variety of clothing styles; some he'd never seen before except on TV shows. Two girls were wearing brightly colored skirts, another pair was wearing dark pants and a knit sweater, and a couple of kids were in shorts and t-shirts. *Wow, they must be freezing!* he thought to himself.

"Greetings, children," a tall and friendly-looking elf called out to them. "Welcome to our snowy home! We are glad you found your way here. And thank you, cousin gnomes, for getting them here so safely."

Hudson sometimes got shy when meeting new people and stepped behind his sister. Tori was three years older and had more practice talking to strangers.

"Hello, I'm Tori," she said confidently. "And this is my brother Hudson. And this is Malcolm and Seamus, our captain."

"And I am Jaquin," the elf replied, his brown eyes twinkling as he smiled warmly. "And you are most welcome. These children also just arrived. We were making our way to the great hall to warm up with some hot cocoa. All will be explained there. Please, gather your bags and join us. We have plenty of food and blankets, so you can leave those things safely behind."

The children came over and began helping with their things. The one in shorts shivered. "Tengo frío!"

Tori looked over to him, not understanding the words he said, but recognizing he was cold. "Oh goodness, you must be freezing!" Suddenly, she remembered the magic rock she had packed from the Land of Fire. "Oh, I know! I have just the thing for you." She pulled the rock from her bag and offered it to him. "Here, hold it. It will warm you up."

He looked at her blankly. "No comprendo." She pantomimed holding the rock and warming up. He still didn't understand. She took the rock and put it directly in his hands. His eyes lit up in understanding as it began to warm his body. "Ahhhh," he said. "Es mágico."

Tori guessed what he was saying and knew at least one word in Spanish. "Sí! Es mágico!"

The boy thanked her. "Gracias, señorita. Me llamo José." Tori guessed he was saying his name was José. "I'm Tori," she replied. "Nice to meet you, José." José ran back to his other friend, who was also in shorts, and they began to hand the stone back and forth to each other as it warmed up their bodies.

"Well, that was a handy thing to have for our trip," she said to Malcolm.

"It sure was," he replied. "I recognized that gnome walking with them. He lives in the jungles of Ecuador, so that's where they must be from. It's near the equator, so a whole lot warmer there than it is here at the Pole!"

"Wow," Hudson chimed in on the conversation. "From the equator. They came a long way to get here." He had a new respect for all the children here, including himself. They'd all traveled a long way from home to come to this strange place.

"Are they here for the same reason as us?" he asked.

"Yes, I think so," Malcolm replied. "The gnome council is made up of gnomes from all around the world. We all learned of the prophecy, and the whole world has been affected by the earthquakes and storms. It wasn't just your country where the government collapsed, leaving people alone and afraid. This happened everywhere, all at once."

Seeing these children from around the world made things hit home for Tori in a way that hadn't before. She spoke slowly, "I know they said this happened everywhere, but I didn't really know, if you know what I mean. But now I really, really know. Wow. It is so awful."

Malcolm thought back to his ruined home. "Yeah, it is."

"That's why we are here, though!" he exclaimed, changing his tone. "To do something about it! You, these other children, the gnomes, the elves. We all want to find out how to help. So, let's look forward instead of backwards."

They finished gathering up their things and followed Jaquin and the other elves down the stone path.

Hudson and Tori knew they were underground, but as they walked on the path, they'd never have guessed it. There were trees filled with little birds chirping and bouncing around, looking for pine seeds in the snow. The ceiling looked very much like a sky, though not quite like the real sky, since it had pearly reflections of rainbows in the clouds that drifted past. There was no direct source of light, like the sun, but it was still quite bright and cheery. The air smelled crisp and cold, fresh like the day after a good snowstorm.

The path was well-maintained with no ice. It was lined with black metal lights that must have illuminated it at night. "I wonder how they know day from night here, being underground?" Hudson mused as he looked at the path lights.

"Ah, that's just a bit of old magic," Malcolm replied. "The light mimics the light on the surface, mirroring the days and nights. Right now, we're in summer, so you'll find it's light pretty much all the time up here at the North Pole. But I bet in the winter, these lights come in handy. It's only light for a couple of hours each day in the winter."

"And how does it snow underground?" he asked, curious about this new world.

"Well, my lad," Seamus chimed in, "it's a bit like a snow globe. It's a closed system; the weather just shakes itself up from time to time to refresh the snow. Shake the snow globe, and then everything looks crisp and fresh again. You'll find the rules of the surface don't quite apply when you get below ground."

"The rules?" Hudson wasn't sure what rules he meant. "Like traffic rules?"

"Oh no," Seamus laughed. "We'll always need traffic rules so we don't run into each other. Every good Captain follows those rules. I mean the rules of how things work. Like gravity, weather, you know, the basics. Under here, deep in the Earth, things have their own way of operating. Especially gravity. It really can get a little bizarre at the poles." He gave Hudson a wink, while Hudson wrinkled his forehead, wondering what he meant.

Seamus continued, "You'll see soon enough. It may seem like magic, but what's magic anyway? Just a word someone made up."

Hudson shrugged his shoulders, still a bit confused. He started to tune into the conversations around him, which were equally confusing. The children were from all over the world and spoke different languages. He couldn't understand a thing anyone was saying, but the elves all seemed to. They chatted back and forth with the kids in a cheerful, friendly tone. Which was good, because the tone from the children seemed a bit worried and anxious.

Tori also picked up on the anxiety, though she couldn't understand the languages. The children spoke in quiet voices, looking around them with wonder but also worry. She was also feeling that same mix of emotions and was a little mad about it.

Here she was, at the North Pole, the magical place of elves, toys, and Santa. It should be all the things that are joyful and jolly. Ahead, she saw cheerful buildings that looked like a village of decorated gingerbread houses. The windows had bright red and green shutters, and the wood-sided walls were decorated with beautiful geometric patterns painted in white, gold, and silver.

They had steep roofs covered with crisp snow and icicles hanging from the eaves. As they got closer to the village, the pine trees were decorated with glass balls and tinsel. She knew it was the middle of June, but she felt like she was walking into a Christmas painting. And that's why it felt strange. At home, it was the middle of June.

It was hotter than it had ever been; they'd had earthquakes and tornadoes, and they didn't have any power or internet. She thought of her friends Julie, Amy, and Madi, wondering if they were okay. How were her parents? Had there been more earthquakes? What did this prophecy mean anyways? Her mind took her to so many places of worry that it almost took the joy out of walking in this magical wonderland.

But just as she started spiraling into worry and doubt, she got pegged in the back of the head by a snowball.

"What the..." she cried out, looking around to see where it had come from.

A small army of elves emerged from behind the trees.

"You can't come to the North Pole without playing in the snow!" one called out, while another in a striped pink and purple hat lobbed a snowball at Hudson's stomach.

"Snowball fight!" Hudson grinned and swooped down to make a snowball.

Tori jumped out of the way of a ball flying her way from the left and knelt to make her own pile of snow ammunition. She was surprised that the snow was not icy cold. It felt cold to the touch but didn't sting her bare skin. And it made perfect snowballs. Tight, compact, and perfectly round. She threw a snowball at her brother.

"Hah! Got you, Hudson!" Before he could respond, Malcolm threw one at her. "Take that!" He laughed and then hid behind Seamus to escape the retaliation snowball that he knew would be coming his way.

They all laughed as children, elves, and gnomes lobbed balls of snow at each other. Many missed their marks and hit the trees around them, knocking fresh snow onto the ground. Birds flew up out of the trees, and squirrels scolded the children with their loud chatter.

Laughter rang out, echoing between the buildings like sleigh bells. Seamus lost his hat in the scuffle, and Hudson saw to his great surprise that he was bald underneath. He had a great, long beard of gray-white, but the top of his head was as pink and shiny as a bowling ball. "Seamus!" he called out, picking up his hat.

Seamus looked mortified and grabbed his blue pointed hat, quickly putting it back on his head. "Thank ye kindly, Master Hudson, I'll be needing that please." After getting his hat secured, he then threw three snowballs in quick succession, hitting Malcolm squarely on the backside. Hudson laughed out loud as Malcolm jumped and turned around, scowling at Seamus.

The fight was interrupted by a loud bell chiming seven times. It was as loud as a church bell, but it had the beautiful tone of a sleigh bell, tinkling magically with each chime. The children stopped to listen, and Tori noticed two great wooden doors open on the building closest to them.

"Ah! It is time," Jaquin called out, putting on a slightly more serious face. "Let's go, my friends. It's time for our meeting." A group of elves came outside the building, greeting the children and gnomes as they entered the building.

As Hudson walked up to the door, he saw a friendly-looking elf dressed in green. "Are we going to meet Santa now? Is he going to lead this meeting?" he asked.

The elf replied, "I'm afraid not, though I'm sure he would have loved meeting all of you. It's not every day we have visitors here!"

He frowned. "But Santa is out traveling the world right now, delivering gifts to children who lost everything in the earthquakes. Our toy supply is not yet up to Christmas levels, but it was the least we could do."

"Wow," Hudson replied, "That is nice of him. I'm bummed we won't meet him, but of course, Santa is out helping people. That's what Santa does, isn't it?"

The elf smiled proudly, "Yes, it sure is. This mission is a special one, but Santa loves to take little working holidays in the summer, spreading a bit of Christmas cheer. Honestly, he's out in your world more often than you think. Wherever you see a person doing something kind for no reason, or giving a gift just to make someone smile, Santa is probably nearby. You've probably even seen him yourself, but didn't realize who he was. Just thought it was a friendly old guy who looked like Santa. It's funny, you humans see so much, and then you don't see anything at all. Magic is right in front of you, but you seldom notice it."

"Oh, I notice tons of things," Hudson said, and it was true. If there were one person who would see Santa, it would probably be Hudson.

As he walked into the hall, Hudson noticed more than a little bit of magic right in front of him. The lights inside the room were floating! Instead of lights hanging from the ceiling or on the walls, there were floating candles that started near the floor and went up in a dome, up to a center point in the middle of the room. At that point was a glowing six-pointed star, shining down on the whole group. It was suspended about 10 feet from the ceiling, but with no wires or cables. He suddenly understood what Seamus was talking about earlier about magic and gravity.

"Cool," he said to the elf, who grinned and then left to help some other elves. He saw kids flocking to a large wooden table on the right. He followed and saw that every inch of the table was covered with food, and not just any food. Cookies, cakes, chocolate, candy canes, caramels, donuts, and other candies were piled high on the table.

"Dinner is served!" Malcolm called out, gleefully filling a small plate with lemon tarts and chocolate donuts. "The elves do love their sweets."

"So do I!" said Tori as she filled up a plate. She found a pitcher of cold milk to go with her cakes and cookies. Hudson also filled his plate high, choosing chocolate chip cookies, salted caramels, a brownie, and a mug of hot chocolate.

Before they had time to wonder where to sit, several tables came floating into the great room and settled into the middle. They were quickly followed by a few dozen chairs that organized themselves neatly at the table.

"Oh wow," Tori said in awe. "That is great timing."

Jaquin stood near the front and called out in a booming voice, "Help yourselves and take your seats, my friends. I'm sure you must be hungry after your long journeys. Enjoy the feast! We'll get started shortly."

Silence descended over the hall as everyone filled their stomachs with sweet treats and cocoa. It was warm inside, and Tori and Hudson took off their coats. José, who Tori had given her magic warming rock, came over and gave the stone back. "Muchas gracias, Tori," he thanked her. "Sure, no problem!" Tori replied. "It is much warmer in here than outside."

He went back to join his friends, and Tori put the magic stone in her pocket. "Magic is pretty handy," she said to herself.

"It sure is," Malcolm replied. "Honestly, I wish you humans would start remembering your magic. Things would be a lot nicer up there if more people found their magic again, like you did."

Tori looked surprised. Last year, she had discovered with the help of some wonderful, but scary fairies, that she had magic. She was able to unlock magical doors and use her heart to light a fire.

"Do other people have magic, too?" Tori asked Malcolm. "For some reason, I thought you had picked me because I was special."

"Of course you're special, Tori!" he replied. "You wouldn't be here right now if you weren't, and no one else could have done what you did for the Phoenix. But loads of humans have magic inside them. You've just forgotten how to see it. You could do so much more with your hearts than you can with your minds, but all they teach you in school is to use your minds. You could create a whole new world if they just started to teach you how to read your heart and use your magic. If they taught you to talk to the trees instead of math and spelling. It's a real shame, to be honest, what they teach in school. They don't even teach you about gardening!"

Tori knew that gnomes loved to garden, and they could talk to the trees and animals. She agreed it was a shame they didn't teach gardening in school. Learning to grow food was as valuable as learning math or spelling.

"I never thought about it that way," she said thoughtfully. "I guess because I only know what I know. And I don't know of any school that teaches how to talk to the trees."

"Exactly!" Malcolm said, a little disappointed. "A basic skill we teach all gnome children. Oh, wouldn't it be grand if we could send human children to our gnome schools in the woods? You'd be so much happier, I can guarantee it. Our children don't learn anything in books, but they still become so much wiser than their parents."

Tori had never heard an adult talk about kids being wise, but it made her think about the prophecy.

"The children will lead the way," she mused quietly, starting to think about what the words might mean.

She had just started to ask Malcolm a question about the prophecy when the enchanting bells they'd heard before rang three long notes. The hall quieted as they saw Jaquin standing in the front of the room on a raised platform. He was accompanied by two gnomes and three elves on either side.

"Sorry, my dear," Malcolm said to Tori, standing up. "This is my cue. If you'll please excuse me." Malcolm went up to the front and stood next to the two other gnomes. Tori wondered if Malcolm was a bit more important than he let on, if he was standing in front of the large crowd that had gathered.

A hundred elves now stood around the tables, and a few more children and gnomes had filtered in.

"Greetings, old friends and new," Jaquin said kindly, surveying the room. "It is a rare day indeed for us all to be standing here, human, gnome, and elf. Why, I can't remember this happening in all my 300 years. A rare day, indeed, but then again it is a strange time, isn't it?" He added the last bit in a somber tone.

"To all of you who live on the surface, please let me first start with my deepest sympathy. I know how hard the last few days have been. So much loss. So much hardship." Tori looked around and could see many people's eyes start to glisten with tears. She knew she'd had it pretty lucky at their house, and wondered what others had gone through.

After a pause of quiet respect, Jaquin continued. "I know how hard it has been for some of you to make this journey. Even in our peaceful underground world, we have felt the effects of the Earth's shaking. The center of the village was protected by magic, but we lost many buildings on the outskirts. The ceiling itself ripped open, and it took a considerable amount of magic to mend the tear." He nodded in gratitude to a group of elves in the corner.

"We are grateful you have all had the courage to come here in these challenging times. And we are grateful to our brothers, the gnomes, for finding the lost prophecy of the Weavers." He nodded deeply to Malcolm, who blushed at the recognition.

"This," he continued, as Malcolm pulled out the scroll he'd been keeping in his pocket, "is why we are all here. To reconnect with the Weavers, our lost brothers and sisters. To find answers. And hopefully, to find a way forward, for all of us."

Malcolm walked up to Jaquin and handed him the scroll. "Here you go, brother," he said in a deep and serious voice. "The gnome council is glad to present this sacred scroll, and we look to our collective efforts to find the way forward."

"Thank you, brother," Jaquin responded, bowing slightly as he took the scroll.

Hudson whispered to Tori, "This is very serious. I didn't know Malcolm could do serious. He's always smiling and laughing." Tori nodded in agreement.

Jaquin took the scroll and turned back to the group. "Many of you have already heard this prophecy, but some have not. It was written by the Weavers. They are elves just like me, but they were more interested in contemplating the mysteries of life than in making toys and candy canes. A long time ago, they left our village at the North Pole and retreated to the Crystal Caves of Contemplation. There, they could tune into the deep rhythms of the Earth and the stars, and they began to weave the Tapestry of Life. The Fates, some might call them, but they were only creating what already was, giving form to the magic of the Universe." He paused, as if remembering a story from his childhood.

"We used to visit the Weavers often, but as they went deeper into the mysteries of life, they found it harder to come out of their meditations to talk to us. Even their language changed as they began to speak only words of mystery and prophecy. A mist formed around their caves that made it harder and harder to find the entrance. Eventually, the mists descended completely, and we could no longer find the way to see our kin. It's sad because they're still family, but we understand how important their work is. They rarely venture out of the caves now, only if they get sick or need a break from their contemplations. It's been a hundred years since we last saw a Weaver, but I have a feeling that is about to change. It's no coincidence that the mists began to lighten in the last two days, after this prophecy was discovered. I believe they are expecting you."

Jaquin unrolled the scroll and read the prophecy to the group, his voice loud and serious.

And a time of great stress and strain in humanity will come, and the world will also feel that strain. The Earth will crack and buckle, and great cities will fall. Storms will sweep the seas and the forests, washing away the old ways of greed and power. Governments will crumble, and the old will look to the young to lead them into the future. From the ashes of the Phoenix, a new epoch will be born. A time of peace and harmony. A time of love and light. And the young will lead the way.

Hudson and Tori had heard it a few times already, but for most in the room, it was the first time. Tori saw José's eyes widen as his gnome friend translated the words. Quiet exclamations came from the other children, who looked around at each other.

After a pause, Jaquin said the last line one more time, with deep feeling. *"And the young will lead the way."*

The hundred elves gathered in the hall all turned to face the children.

And began to clap.

They weren't clapping at Jaquin up on stage, or Malcolm, who was putting the scroll back in his pocket. They were clapping at the children. The children who had come there from all around the world. The children who had left their parents and homes and traveled through underground rivers and rapids. Who were probably afraid but trying so hard to be brave and strong. They were clapping for them.

The children looked around in awe, at each other, and themselves. And as the clapping continued, something happened inside every one of those children's hearts.

The fear and anxiety began to dissolve, replaced by hope. Smiles began to spread across their faces as their hearts began to light up with possibility. As they looked around at the elves clapping for them, believing they were the key to the future, they began to believe it themselves. They felt empowered and strong. And in that moment, they didn't feel like children at all. They felt like champions. One child stood up, and then another, and they all began to clap. For each other, for themselves. For being there and showing up in the moment that really counted.

The hall was filled with the sound of clapping, and it soared to the top of the ceiling with each child's heart. Gnomes, elves, and children began to hug each other, as tears fell from their eyes. They had been held in from the worry and fear about all that had happened, but now in this moment, they realized they were exactly where they had meant to be. And not only that, it had been prophesied!

In a rare moment of sibling love, Tori hugged Hudson, and Hudson hugged her back. "I'm glad you're here, little brother," she said.

As the clapping and hugging began to die down, Jaquin took charge of the room again.

"Thank you all for that beautiful display of love and hope. Just what we needed in these times of troubles. So now that we're all here, and we are all on the same page, what do you say, shall we give our dear kin, the Weavers, a visit? Let's find out how you beautiful young humans can lead the way to peace and harmony again!"

Cheers erupted from the crowd, as "Yes!" and "Let's go!" were shouted enthusiastically in many languages.

Malcolm returned to the group and hugged Hudson and Tori, saying excitedly, "Let's go find the Weavers!"

* * *

Before everyone ran off to find the mystical elves lost to time, there was some practicality to attend to. The children and gnomes were exhausted! The North Pole Elves knew this and had been working hard in the background to make sure beds had been made and stocked with warm, cozy blankets.

Since it was summer at the North Pole, the sky didn't get very dark, but Tori and Hudson didn't need a sunset to know it was time for bed. After the excitement of meeting the elves and talking about the prophecy wore off, they were soon yawning so loudly it was almost embarrassing. Except that everyone else was yawning too.

Malcolm, who had been to the North Pole before, expertly guided them through the village of quaint gingerbread-like houses. He brought them to a finely decorated cottage near the edge of the village. There was candy cane striped trim around the windows and festive garland over the door. The front door had a beautiful sun and moon carved into the wood, and shooting stars carved into the frame.

Once inside, a cozy fire was already burning in the fireplace. Four wooden rocking chairs with intricately carved images of reindeer, polar bears, and foxes sat in a circle by the fire. It was one large room, with a kitchenette at one end and a sleeping area at the other. Four wooden bunk beds had been made up with brightly colored sheets and blankets.

A small wash closet by the kitchen had a sink, toilet, and shower. Tori stopped in there first, happy to wash off the dirt of traveling from her face. There were four mugs of hot cocoa waiting for them on a table, with little dishes of marshmallows and peppermint sticks to add if they wanted.

They all sat down to enjoy hot cocoa, when Tori remembered the journal. "Hudson! We need to write Mom and Dad, and make sure they're okay. That illusion we saw on the river was just so real."

He ran over to his bag and pulled the journal out. He opened it and saw they had written back to his message from last night.

Tori and Hudson, Let us know you're okay as soon as you read this. We had terrible thunderstorms today. Huge winds and flooding, but we're okay. The radio told us there was a lot of damage to cities near rivers. We were worried since you're on a river. Write as soon as you can.

Love you, Mom

Tori read over his shoulder, getting through the words faster than him. "Wow, Malcolm," she said. "Check this out. There were big storms today on the surface. I wonder if they caused the tidal wave."

She took out a pen to write back to their mom.

"Hey Mom, we're safe. We're at the North Pole! Can you believe it? But no Santa Claus. He's off helping kids around the world. Anyways, we had some crazy times on the river, but we're doing great.

Love you, Tori

They put the book back and talked about the storms as they drank cocoa. Malcolm wondered if the Veil of illusion wasn't entirely illusion after all. Hudson shuddered at the thought, glad to have read that his parents and the farm were okay. He tried to follow the conversation, but he was so tired he couldn't even finish his drink, delicious as it was.

With a huge yawn, he kicked off his shoes and crawled into the bottom bunk in the corner.

"I'm out!" he said. "I don't think I can keep my eyes open for another minute, even with the talk of storms and tidal waves, and daylight streaming into the windows."

"Ah," Malcolm replied, going over to the window. "Good point. Here, I'll fix that. Everyone, get settled. Hudson's right. Enough talk for the night, we should get some sleep." He shooed Tori and Seamus to their beds and then pulled a heavy red velvet curtain over the window. It was so thick that it completely blacked out the light from outside, and the only light remaining was from the fire. The simple cottage transformed into a cozy, warm, dark space, perfect for a good night's sleep.

Now, it might be imagined that a child visiting the North Pole would have dreams filled with sugar plum fairies, gingerbread cookies, and all the things in children's stories, but those stories were not written when the world had gone quite so upside down as it had for Tori and Hudson. Their dreams were not cheerful sugar cookies and candy canes. They were filled with earthquakes, floods, fire, and fear.

Seamus, who had always been a light sleeper, could see the two tossing and turning and felt great sympathy for them. "Ay," he whispered to himself, "these poor children being born in such a time as this. I wish we could have given them the peaceful childhood I had." As he spoke, Hudson cried out and sat up, his eyes still closed. He murmured something, reached out a hand, and then lay back down.

As Seamus watched over them, he could see something shift in their dreams. A calmness filled the room, and the twitching stopped. The children's breathing eased and settled into soft snores like a cat purring. Filled himself with that sense of calm, Seamus lay down and relaxed into a much-needed rest.

For the first time in what felt like weeks, they all had a deep and peaceful sleep.

* * *

* * *

Ten

Finding the Weavers

The next morning, everyone woke abruptly when Malcolm pulled open the curtain, bright light streaming in through the window.

"Geez, Malcolm!" Tori complained, sitting up and stretching. "You think you could give us a little warning there! That sunlight is bright enough to burn my eyeballs!"

Malcolm laughed, glad to see the children refreshed. He stoked the fire and put out fresh mugs of cocoa he'd brought from the Great Hall.

Hudson was the first to get to his mug and added three peppermint sticks. "It's like a Starbucks Peppermint Mocha, without the coffee, of course." Hudson grimaced at the idea of coffee, and Tori stuck her tongue out at him, as she was becoming a big fan.

"I had the CRAZIEST dreams," he mused as he sipped his cocoa.

"Me, too!" Tori added, as she put a dozen marshmallows and caramel drizzle into hers.

"They were awful at first," her eyes darkened as she remembered the scenes of destruction. "But then, I don't know how to explain it, but something else came into my dream. Or someone."

"Yeah," Hudson said thoughtfully. "Me, too. Like they came in through the back door of my head. Then the dream started to change."

Malcolm was intrigued. "Did you see them? What did they look like?"

"No," Hudson said slowly, "Not exactly, but I could feel them there. Like they were standing just behind my eyes. But I knew if I turned around, I wouldn't have been able to see them. But I felt them, and they were changing my dream. At first, it was a total nightmare, but then a haze came, like a cloud covering everything, and it dissolved all the scary things. And they started to turn into nicer things."

Tori interrupted, "Yeah! Me, too! At first, I was dreaming that my friend's houses had all collapsed, and fires were burning in the cities. And then a rain came and put out the fires, and flowers started to grow up where the ash had been. And then I saw...I don't know how to describe it. It was like threads of light going from house to house, reconnecting all the broken bricks and stones. They started to move back together, and the houses began to build again."

"Threads of light, did you say?" Seamus pulled at his beard thoughtfully.

Hudson jumped in, "That's what I dreamt too! Strings were going between all the broken trees and smashed roads, and the strings were pulling things back together again. I could almost feel like the person, or whatever it was, was the one doing it. They were the ones creating the strings. But for me, they weren't light, they were every color of the rainbow. The blue ones fixed the rivers, the green ones were fixing the trees that had fallen, and the brown ones were fixing the houses."

"My word," Malcolm said, "I think the Weavers visited your dreams! I think they were the ones changing the story. This is good news indeed. I am sure they won't be so hard to find, now that they've reached out to you. I'd bet they've reached out to all the children here, showing you how to fix what is broken."

"The Weavers?" Hudson asked, "Like the elves we are here to find were in our dreams? And not just our dreams, but everyone's dreams? How is that even possible?"

"Welcome to the North Pole, Hudson," Malcolm winked at him. "Here, everything is possible."

After finishing his cocoa, Hudson wanted to check on the journal. "Maybe the Weavers came to the real world, and not just our dreams!" he said, as he handed the book to Tori, who was sitting on the bed.

She opened the book to the page they'd written on last night. "Yeah, maybe everything has gotten better overnight!" There was a new entry from her mom. She read it quickly to herself.

> *Tori, I'm so glad you're ok. Your dad got some news this morning. The ice rink you go to collapsed in the storm yesterday. There were a lot of people who were using it as a shelter. They didn't make it. I'm so sorry. I almost didn't want to tell you, but you had to know. We love you and we are so proud of you for being brave and courageous.*
>
> *Love, Mom and Dad*

Tori closed the book in silence. Hudson hadn't seen the page, and she intended to keep it that way.

"Did they write back?" Hudson asked, his face hopeful. She looked at him for a moment, and then told him the only thing that felt right to her. "No, they didn't."

She sat on the bed, looking down at the floor. Malcolm looked at her with a penetrating gaze. Finally, he said, "Well, Hudson, we may not have heard from them, but let's keep the hope. Go on and change into some fresh clothes, and I'll wash up the dishes."

Tori put the book away and was quiet while she changed. Hudson didn't notice her silence. He was excited about his dreams the night before and the idea of going on an adventure. But Malcolm knew something was wrong and went over to her while Hudson was putting his bag together.

"I'm sorry, my friend," he said, his eyes crinkling in compassion. She nodded, her eyes speaking without words, as she put on her shoes and coat.

She stood up, with a determined look on her face. "Let's go find these mysterious Weavers," she said and walked to the door of their cozy cottage.

The four companions stepped outside into a cheerful sunny morning. As they walked back to the Great Hall, Hudson had lots of questions.

"First of all," he asked Malcolm, "How do you lose a group of elves? This place doesn't seem THAT big."

Before Malcolm could answer, Hudson peppered him with more questions. "And how far away do you think these crystal caves are? And what is the mist that hid them? Is it like the mist we saw on the river? Or like the mist in my dreams? Have you ever met them? Are they nice or weird? Are we all going together? How long do you think it will take us?"

The four of them were back in the hall before Malcolm had a chance to attempt even one answer, so he simply said with a smile, "Good questions, Hudson, you should ask Jaquin."

As they walked inside, the sound of laughing voices and the smell of breakfast filled the air. Tori counted almost 50 children and gnomes, all looking cheerful and well-rested.

Malcolm guided them over to breakfast that had been set up on the large table in the back of the room. Pancakes, waffles, and crepes were piled high along with fruits, whipped cream, chocolate spreads, and bottles of maple syrup. They filled their plates and sat down to eat. Just as Seamus was polishing off his fourth pancake, the head elf went up to the front of the room and rang a large bell to get everyone's attention.

"Good morning," Jaquin called out to everyone, "I hope you all slept well and had the sweetest dreams, and are now enjoying an even sweeter breakfast." The children nodded appreciatively at the elves' breakfast selection. "Today is the day we go in search of the Weavers! When everyone's done eating, please join me outside, and we shall begin the quest! Don't worry about clearing your plates, not today. Today is a day for adventure!"

Everyone jumped up at once, excited to go in search of the Weavers. The children had all been visited in their dreams and were eager to find the mysterious dream walkers who could turn nightmares into joy. They put their jackets on to go outside into the cold. Tori was glad to see that the kids who had been in shorts yesterday were outfitted with pants, coats, and gloves. She was also happy to have her magic stone in her pocket to keep her hands warm.

They went outside and gathered in a large group around Jaquin. Once everyone had assembled, he spoke to the crowd. "Now you may be wondering how we're all going to travel in such a big group. We're not!"

There was a surprised murmur in the crowd. Weren't they all trying to find the same cave and the same Weavers?

"You see," he continued, "there's no one simple way to the Cave of Contemplation. There are many paths, but they all lead to the same place. One path goes to the right here," he pointed to a dirt path on his right that led into a deep and thick forest.

"One to the left." He pointed to a gravel road winding away from them. It went up a hill between large stones and boulders and then towards a steep mountain face.

"And one behind us here." He turned to show a paved path that looked

113

bright and cheerful, leading out of the village and towards a sunny field. "Oh, don't be fooled by that one, it is the toughest path of them all," he said gravely.

"Then there's the path that goes back the way you came." They turned around and looked at the lake, confused by his words. The boats sat on the beach, and the archway they had come through was in the distance. Tori wondered to herself, *How could the path to the Weavers be there? They'd already come that way.*

"You can take whatever path you want. They will all lead you to the Weavers, or they won't, and they will lead you right back to where you started."

Now Tori was truly confused, and looked to Malcolm to see if he knew anything that would be helpful. Hudson scratched his head and looked around to see if one path looked better than the other.

Malcolm grinned, always seeing the sunny side of things. "Well, if they all get us to where we want to go, I guess we should pick the one that looks most fun!" Tori started to eye the bright and cheery road ahead of them, but then remembered what Jaquin had said about it being the hardest path. Hudson looked towards the trees. "To me, the woods are always the most fun! We should go that way." He pointed to the deep and dark forest.

Tori started thinking of the poison ivy, brambles, and thick undergrowth in her woods at home. But she did know woods, since her house was surrounded by them. Going back the way they'd come seemed annoying, as did climbing up rocks, so she shrugged her shoulders and agreed.

"Alright then, let's go that way." They looked around and saw other children making decisions about which way to go.

Jaquin interrupted their discussions. "The elves can't join you, my friends, though the gnomes can, and they bring luck and magic wherever they go. The mists blocked our path a long time ago. We can't find our brothers and sisters, no matter how hard we try. We hope they will clear for you, and that the prophecy and the tied dreams you had last night are good omens. The Veil of Illusion cleared for you, so let us hope that these mists do as well."

His voice became serious. "But be warned. The mists are like dreams that never came to light. They are realities that you could get lost in. You must stick to your truth and remember who you are. Follow your heart and not your mind, and you will find the way through."

With that mysterious warning, Jaquin and the elves left them to their choices. Tori, Hudson, Malcolm, and Seamus headed off towards the forest.

Two other groups joined them. There were two sisters from Austria, and a sister and brother from India. They couldn't speak each other's languages, but the gnomes translated. Gnomes seemed to know everything, from human languages to how to find their way in the woods. The sisters, named Julia and Gretchen, lived in a picturesque valley in the Austrian Alps. They had escaped the worst of the earthquakes, but the storms caused a massive flash flood in the valley. It took out most of their village and all the roads. Their family lost their home, and was living in a tent in the woods. A gnome had found them playing by an old oak tree and invited them to come on the journey.

The Indian siblings, Chetan and Jiya, were from Northern India, near a big fault line. They'd had 10 huge earthquakes, one after the other. It destroyed their city, and there was no water or electricity for anyone. Their house had miraculously survived, and their parents had invited many neighbors to stay with them. Jiya had met the gnomes in the family garden the year before. They'd built a friendship planting and growing things together.

Each family had their own story, but they were all tied together by the earthquakes and storms, by the fear and worry for their families, and by the hope that they'd be able to find the Weavers.

Gnomes weren't just good at languages and gardening; they were also a cheery, joyful sort. Even as the forest began to close in on the group, Malcolm kept everyone entertained with jokes and stories. He'd tell a joke, and then translate it for each group. Soon, all the children were laughing.

But as they walked deeper into the forest, the bright sunshine, along with the laughter, began to fade in the darkening trees.

Malcolm spoke less, and the birds stopped chirping. The sound of laughter was replaced by an eerie quiet. The trees grew still, as the wind stopped moving even the top tree branches. The silence thickened as they walked deeper into the woods.

The path still stretched out before them, but it grew darker and grayer. The dirt started to turn from brown to gray. The rocks became gray. Even the trees began to lose their green. All the color in the woods was fading and turning to gray.

Tori looked over to Hudson's tie-dyed hoodie. "Hudson, your shirt's gone gray! All the color is gone!"

He looked down at the rainbow colored sweatshirt. The swirls were there, but not the color. He looked at his hands. They were gray, not tan. Malcolm's red hat was gray, and so was Tori's brown hair. "We are all gray!" It was like they'd stepped out of a world of color and into a black and white movie.

Everyone stopped to look around at each other. And that is when they started to notice the mist.

It descended on them like a thick, wet blanket. Unlike the mists in the river, there were no images or illusions. It was a dense fog, and it made the cold air feel even colder. Tori shivered in her coat and reached into her pocket to hold her magical stone from the Land of

Fire. She remembered the friendly face of Charlie, a gallywomp she'd met there, but it seemed like a lifetime ago. The thick mist blocked out their view of the trees, and they could only see the path ahead of them.

"We have to keep going," Tori said, determined. "We have to find the Weavers so we can figure out how to fix the world." Her mind went back to the news of the ice rink. She started to walk forward again, into the gray, and the others followed.

They trudged through the growing mist, feet dragging. It weighed on them, physically. Their shoulders started to droop. Their mouths turned downward into frowns. Their legs became heavy, and then they stopped walking altogether.

Hudson looked at Tori, "I feel so heavy." His eyes, normally a bright brown, were gray and sad.

Even cheerful Malcolm was being affected. "What's the point?" he said glumly and sat down on a log. "What can one little gnome do in the world?"

Tori joined him on the log, looking down at the ground, as the heavy, dark mist thickened around them. She felt a growing sense of oppression and hopelessness. She looked ahead at the path going through the forest. The fog was getting so thick that it was starting to disappear from view. She looked back from where they'd come. She could see sunshine in the distance, beckoning them to turn around and go back.

"Yeah, maybe you're right, Malcolm," she sighed. "What is the point? We're just a bunch of kids. We can't do anything. If those magical elves haven't found their way through these mists, why do we think we can? We aren't special."

The other children had also stopped walking. Chetan and Jiya sat down by Tori, looking fallen and dejected. The colors of their bright clothing had turned a dull gray. Gretchen stood nearby and kicked the gray soil with her gray shoe.

Hudson tried to keep walking forward, but he couldn't see two feet in front of them. He turned around, and the way back was clear as day. "There's no way we can go on. This mist is getting heavier and heavier." He took a deep breath. "I can hardly breathe, it's so heavy. What are we going to do?"

Gretchen sighed, speaking a bit of English. "We go back?"

They sat there, dejected. There was no way forward. Even if they'd wanted to keep going, the mist was so thick the path had completely disappeared. But even if they could see the path, they had lost the will to keep going. The mist had taken away their hope, like it had taken away the color in their clothes.

Malcolm shuffled his feet in the dirt. "Even the elves said they couldn't find a way to the Weavers. Maybe it was a fool's errand to think we could do something that they hadn't been able to do for a hundred years."

When Malcolm mentioned the elves, Tori tried to remember what Jaquin had said back in that sunny plaza outside of the cheerful gingerbread-looking village of the North Pole. All she could see and feel around her was darkness and gray, but she knew he'd said something important. Something that would help them in the mists. Then she remembered it.

"Follow your heart, not your mind," she said out loud to the group. "That's what Jaquin said."

She remembered something from her quest last summer about the magic in her heart opening the magic door at the castle. She had created magic by believing in her heart she could do it, not by anything she did with her mind.

"But we can't even see the path." Hudson complained.

But Tori understood what Jaquin meant. It wasn't about what her eyes could see, but what her heart told her. She knew what they had to do. "We have to believe we can get through the mist, not just think we can."

She stood up and pointed to her heart as she looked around at the other children. "We have to believe it here. Inside."

Tori closed her eyes so she wouldn't see the mist and the gray. She closed them even tighter, scrunching her face up, to block out even the thought of the mist. And then she came into her heart.

She felt into who she was. Tori. No one fancy, famous, or special, just her. She gave herself a little hug. She did that sometimes. It was like a reassuring pat on the back from herself to herself. Then she created a deep wish in her heart that she could find the Weavers.

She remembered her dream and the Weaver that was behind her, making the threads of light. She felt the hope in that dream, that things could be fixed. She let that hope fill her heart, lighting her internal flame.

She imagined her heart was a candle and could light the way through the darkness. With her eyes closed tight, she let that feeling fill her up. It grew and grew, and then she knew, not with her mind, but with her heart, the way through the mist. With her eyes closed, she could see a brightness to the right of her. She opened her eyes, but still only saw thick fog.

She closed them again and focused on that bright spot. She imagined the mist dissolving, and the light growing. She put her whole heart into it, until she could see it clearly, even though her eyes were still closed.

She opened her eyes once more and looked to the spot she'd seen in her mind. The mists began to dissolve, and a path appeared as a sharp turn to the right. There was a break in the trees, with a narrow path that went through them. "Look, everyone," she called out, pointing to her right. "There's the path! It's just there!"

No one else could see it, still lost in the gray mists. "What are you talking about, Tori?" Hudson called out. "There's nothing there."

"Hudson, close your eyes! Feel the path. Don't look with your eyes, believe with your heart. Feel the hope of the Weavers from your dreams. Let it fill your heart. And then let that hope show you the way."

He closed his eyes. Tori guided him, "Feel the light?"He nodded. "Okay, let it grow in your heart." After a short time, he opened his eyes. They immediately widened in surprise. "I see it!"

"Seamus, Malcolm, do you see it? Tell the others. Believe with their hearts, not their minds."

As the mists faded for Tori and Hudson, they felt bright and hopeful again. Encouraged by their success, the other children closed their eyes to try and feel into their hearts. They came back to that place of hope that had never really left them, but had been hidden by the gray. Tori guided them, helping them to focus on the belief they could find the Weavers.

Once their hearts were filled with belief again, they could also feel the path appear. They opened their eyes, and everyone now saw the path through the trees.

The dark gray mist began to dissolve, and the trees emerged from the thick fog. Then the color returned, first to the children and then to the entire forest. Birds began to chirp, and the sun filtered through the trees. The mist left as mysteriously as it had arrived.

Seamus laughed, filled once again with his normal sense of adventure. "Well, what are you all waiting around for? Let's go!" He walked towards the path, and the others followed, smiles returned to their faces.

The path took them through a dense grove of trees, then opened into a clearing. At the edge of the clearing was an immense mountain, rising sharply in front of them.

"How did we never see that before?" Hudson wondered. It reached as tall as the sky, going all the way to the top of the cavern ceiling. An impenetrable wall of stone stretched to the right and left, but in front of them was a small opening. It was not much taller than a child and only as wide as two children standing shoulder to shoulder. As they walked closer, they realized it was an opening to a cave. From it glowed a faint light, like a beacon calling them home.

"The Crystal Cave of Contemplation," Malcolm said softly. "Not in a thousand Sundays would I have imagined seeing this sight."

They walked towards the massive stone mountain. There wasn't a single crack or rough edge on the face, except that one entrance. The entry was smooth, with no cracks or rough points. It wasn't a natural cave opening. It was shaped like an egg, round and then narrowing at the top. The glow emanating from the cave became brighter and pulsed softly, as if it was sending a Morse code message out to the world. At the top of the entrance, there was a small wooden sign with strange symbols printed on it.

What does it say?' Hudson asked.

Malcolm peered at the sign for a moment and then smiled.

"It's in Old Elvish. It says," and he paused, "Welcome to a New Reality."

"That's quite a claim," Seamus interjected, as he peered into the cave entrance.

Malcolm laughed, "Well, I can't think of any other elves who'd have that for a welcome sign. Friends, I do believe we've found the Weavers!

* * *

The North Passage

* * *

Eleven

What Happened to Gravity?

Julia and Gretchen were the first to enter the cave. They were used to mountains, as were Chetan and Jiya, and walked confidently into the small space. Tori and Hudson were the last to go, looking closely at the cave walls.

They could see why it was called the Crystal Caves. The walls were polished crystal. Mostly clear quartz, but there were also veins of smoky quartz, pink quartz, and amethyst running through. Light emanated from the crystal itself, a bit like it did in the underground rivers, and it created a soft, inviting glow.

Hudson reached out to touch the walls. They were smooth and cool to the touch. "So cool," he awed. He loved rocks and crystals of all kinds. He'd get excited if he found a small geode or a piece of quartz at the lake. Walking through a cave that was all crystal was like hitting the jackpot.

As they went deeper into the cave, the crystal walls appeared to be humming. "What is that?" Tori asked out loud. "Do you hear that?" She looked confused, but everyone nodded in agreement.

"It sounds like a tuning fork," Malcolm said, referring to a metal fork they used to use to tune instruments. It was quiet, but they could all hear it—a low, clear hum emanating from the walls.

"I feel a tingle in my body," Hudson added after a bit. "Are they tuning us?" he asked, only half joking.

"Maybe they are," Malcolm replied. "They can't just let any old frequency into these caves. The Weavers are mystics. They've spent hundreds of years meditating on the very nature of reality. I can't even imagine what that would begin to do to them after a while."

Hudson asked Tori quietly, "Do you think they might be crazy? Like meditating for a hundred years. Could that make someone lose their mind?"

Tori wondered, as well. "I don't know Hudson. But I think we'd better be prepared for anything."

The hum continued, and Tori felt a tingling sensation throughout her whole body. It didn't hurt, but it was quite strange. Her ears were ringing too, as if the hum was vibrating her eardrums. The sound grew louder, and was starting to get uncomfortable, but then abruptly stopped . They had reached a junction in the cave system. There was a tunnel that went to the right and left, and one that continued forward. The path forward was brightly lit and twice the size of the others, so they continued straight.

Soon, they began to hear the sound of music, faint at first. It was a cheerful melody, and what sounded like flutes and bells. The passage got brighter and larger as they walked, and the melody grew louder. They knew they must be close. Then the light, which had been a soft white, changed to rainbow technicolor. It started to swirl. The music picked up, with drums adding some dance beats. The lights swirled in time to the music.

"Fun," Hudson said out loud. "It's like we're walking into an elf dance party!"

As he spoke, the tunnel opened up into a large cavern filled with swirling rainbow lights. They looked up to the ceiling and could see that the source of the light was a giant spinning disco ball. The music brought smiles to everyone's faces, and they looked around to see where it was coming from. They didn't see anyone in the room. The ground was a smooth mirror glass floor, reflecting the lights of the disco but was empty except for their small group. They turned around, looking behind them, and they only saw shiny crystal walls. Then they looked up.

Above them, floating in the air, legs folded in a meditation position, were six elves. One was wearing tie-dye coveralls, playing a drum. Another, in flowing purple robes, played a flute. And another was floating completely upside down, her long hair flowing to the ground. She was playing a set of bells that were chiming even though they were upside down. A fourth had cymbals, and a fifth was softly strumming a guitar. The last had no instruments, her hands on her knees in deep meditation.

The elves were so engrossed in their music that they didn't see the children below them. The children watched, enthralled by elves defying gravity in a swirling disco dance hall deep underground. The elves' eyes were all closed, and yet they somehow kept in perfect harmony with each other. At last, the music slowed, and the disco ball began to slow in time. The elves slowly floated down to the floor, the children watching with their jaws open.

The one that had been upside down turned right side up again as she put her feet onto the mirror glass floor and opened her eyes, looking directly at Hudson.

"Why hello there, young man," she said with a serene smile. "We were just contemplating the beauty of a sunset. It's quite a thing, isn't it? No two ever quite the same."

Hudson didn't know what to think. Were these elves brilliant? Or absolutely mad?

But of course, he also agreed with the elf. "I suppose you're right," he said. "No two ever are the same, are they?"

The Weavers smiled warmly at the children. "Welcome to our humble home. We are glad you found your way past the mists and the tuners. It's a good thing you all have a high frequency, or those tuning crystals can cause quite a headache."

Tori thought of her aunt, who was always going on about crystals and frequencies and high vibrations. She'd been a bit skeptical, but then again, here they were. She'd seen stranger things this week than a tuning crystal.

She looked around at the elves, noticing not a single one dressed or looked the same. Each had their own style. There was the one with the tie-dye overalls, her hair brightly colored, then the one in the purple flowing robes. He was tall and thin. Then there was a short elf, dressed in a serious black suit, next to one with long curly hair dressed in linen pants and a crop top. She thought of most music bands that all had a similar look. These elves looked so different, yet still made beautiful music together.

Her friends all had different styles, too, and she didn't care. Some of the things they liked, she liked, and others she didn't, and it was fine. It didn't make them any less fun to hang out with. She was glad the Weavers were the same way.

The short, serious-dressed one spoke up next, "You are the first to arrive. Let's all go to the Weaving Room. We will get you some refreshments while we see who else finds their way through the mists."

She saw a look of concern on Julia's face. "Don't worry," she assured her. "If they don't find the way through the mists, it will eventually send them back to the North Pole elves. They will either be led here or back to where they started."

"That's good to know. Thank you." Julia said. "It was scary out there in the woods. I'm glad the other children will be okay."

Tori and Hudson looked at each other in surprise. They'd understood everything Julia had said.

"Julia, do you know English?"

Julia looked a bit confused."Not really," she said.

The elf laughed a good-natured laugh. "Oh, silly me," she interrupted them, "I forgot to mention! The tuning you received on the way in. It has a unique effect on human ears." Tori thought of the ringing in her ears. "You should be able to understand each other just fine now, no matter what language you speak."

Hudson's eyes widened. "Cool! Thanks! That saves a lot of language lessons!" He grinned at Chetan, happy he could talk to him now.

The elf guided them quickly and efficiently into a passage ahead of them. They walked through the narrow passage and then entered another cavern, twice as large as the first one and perfectly round. Instead of mirrored glass and clear crystal, it was a warm, golden yellow color.

"The walls are made of citrine," Hudson informed everyone. The elves were impressed with his knowledge of crystals. "I have a pretty big collection at home," he beamed.

The center of the dome was empty, but at the edges were several seating areas. The Weavers led them to one, full of brightly colored pillows and cushions. They were in every shape and size. Some were tie-dyed, some were jungle patterns, and others were wild geometric shapes.

"Sorry, we don't do furniture around here," the tie-dyed elf told them. "But relax and get comfortable. We'll bring some tea out for everyone in just a moment. Clyde, do you want to give them a song while they wait?" Clyde, the elf in purple robes, pulled out his pan flute and smiled at them silently.

The tie-dyed elf explained, "Clyde hasn't spoken in a long time. His language now is music." Clyde walked with them over to the cushions. Everyone found a pillow perfectly sized for them and sat down. Clyde also sat, but they noticed he wasn't actually on the cushion. He floated about two inches above it.

"Do they just ignore gravity down here or something?" Tori mused. Clyde winked at her and shrugged his shoulders. Then he began to play his flute.

They quickly became mesmerized by the music. Though it had no words, it somehow told them a story. It was the story of the forest they'd been in. Hudson wasn't sure how he knew it, but he knew. Each tree had a voice. The flute captured the sound of their limbs swaying in the breeze. It sang of the birds making nests with the branches. Short high-pitched notes were the calls of the hungry baby birds looking for their parents. Then there were the sounds of storms and lazy summer afternoons. Hudson closed his eyes and almost felt like he was there, part of the forest.

The sound of autumn came, the flute playing the sound of leaves falling. The music captured the sound of winter, the quietness of the snow. It was almost silent, but Clyde played a slight whisper on the flute. It was the sound of life continuing, even in the dark winter. Then it began to play the sounds of spring again. The music had completed the full cycle of seasons, and the children had all been transported on that journey.

He stopped, smiled serenely, and bowed to each child. They didn't even think to clap, so moved they had been by the magic of the music. It was like they saw the world in a way they'd never seen it before. The music showed them how all the plants and animals in the forest were connected, and how the seasons connected them in a full circle.

Tori looked around and noticed tea had been placed for them, but she couldn't recall anyone walking by. She picked up her cup and took a small sip. She could taste the different flavors of each kind of leaf and herb, as if the song had sharpened her senses.

After Clyde enjoyed his cup of tea, he began to play another song on his flute. This one transported them to the ocean. It had the waves, the tides, and even the fish and birds that lived there. Tori could almost see the seagull flying over the waves, calling to its friends. The flute captured the sound of each seagull, dipping into the waves.

They all relaxed into their pillows, hoping the music would never end. Clyde finished the piece, ending with a triumphant crash of a wave. This time, the children remembered to clap, and Clyde brought his hands to his heart in gratitude. Standing up, he put his feet back onto the floor and nodded towards a new group of children that had arrived.

* * *

* * *

Twelve

All the Children Arrive

⚜

The group that walked in didn't look like they'd enjoyed their journey to the Crystal Caves. They were soaking wet, their clothes clinging to their skin. Strands of hair stuck to their face Their eyes looked resolute and determined, but exhausted.

The Weavers quickly welcomed the children and gnomes, handing out warm, fluffy towels and mugs of hot tea. Malcolm went over to them to find out what misadventures they'd had trying to find their way.

Tori and Hudson helped exchange wet towels for dry ones while the kids warmed up and dried off. Meanwhile, Malcolm was talking animatedly with another gnome. The gnome was waving his hands, his hat bobbing as he spoke.

Malcolm returned, awe on his face. "Oh, the poor things. But what courage! What tenacity!"

"What happened?" Hudson asked impatiently.

"Well, they went back the way we had come, thinking that it would be the safest way. They thought that going backwards, back to the lake

131

and river they'd been on, would be the easiest way here. But going backwards rarely gives you the same experience." He got a distant look as if remembering a time when he tried to go back on something in life, and it hadn't worked out well for him.

"Anyway," he continued, "they went on the boats back into the lake, but just as they got into the middle, it changed. What had been a calm lake turned into a giant whirlpool! They paddled as hard as they could, but they couldn't row the boats out. They were pulled under the water! Down to the bottom of the Lake!"

Hudson and Tori both gasped.

"But the story didn't end there, thank goodness! Right when they thought all was lost, they were rescued by the Mer creatures. They gave them breathing devices so they could breathe underwater."

The children looked pleased, but Malcolm shook his head and continued. "The children were happy to be saved by the Mer, who took them to their underwater city. But there's a catch. You see, Mers love having visitors to their city, but not for fun and games. They want you to stay and help with all their chores! Sea farming, aquaculture, cooking, cleaning, and they aren't keen on letting their visitors leave once they've come. No, visiting a Mer city is not something I'd recommend at all. They seem to have mixed up the word 'visitor' with the word 'prisoner.' That young girl over there found a secret tunnel. And amazingly, that tunnel led them straight here! They had about 30 Mer creatures chasing after them, but as soon as they crossed the threshold into the crystal cave, the barrier closed behind them. So, they are safe now."

"I always thought mermaids were supposed to be nice," Hudson said.

Tori knew better, having met some less-than-kind magical creatures last year. "I don't think that being a magical creature means you're nice. They're just like humans. Some are nice, and some aren't. I'm sure glad they escaped. I will definitely keep that in mind if I ever get invited to visit a Mer city! Geesh. I hope the other kids didn't have a bad journey up the mountain or through the village."

Clyde played another song to help the new children relax after their harrowing escape. One of the other elves danced rhythmically around them, weaving between the children with grace and ease.

Tori and Hudson spoke a bit with the new children. They were quite relieved to be at the Crystal Cave after their adventure.

Eventually, another group of children and gnomes came in. They had taken the mountain pass. An old, gray-bearded gnome told Malcolm they'd almost turned around. "It was so steep, you see," he said with a thick accent, "we were practically crawling up the mountain. I'm so proud of these young ones, they really stuck it out."

Most of them had scrapes on their knees and hands from scrambling over rocks. One girl had a particularly deep gash on her leg. But they all looked proud to be there. Tori helped the Weavers clean the cuts and put on a healing ointment, while Hudson brought them warm drinks and food.

Finally, the last group of children arrived. They were the ones who had taken the path through the village. The one that Jaquin had said looked easy, but was the hardest one of all.

They seemed deeply shaken by their experience. They looked around, touching everything, almost to see if it was real. "What happened to them?" Tori asked quietly. "It looks as if they aren't sure we are real."

Malcolm, who had taken on the role of group ambassador, went over to talk to a small gnome who had walked in with the children. The Weavers guided the newcomers to a separate area of cushions covered with soft pastel-colored silks. They appeared quite traumatized, and Clyde began to play them peaceful music. It sounded like a lullaby parents would use to soothe a crying baby.

Malcolm came back to report what had happened, shaking his head softly. "Oh, they did have a rough go of it, the darlings. We'd best let them collect themselves for a bit."

"What do you mean?" Hudson asked sympathetically, "Are they okay?"

Malcolm nodded and continued, "They will be, I'm sure, after some grounding tea and gentle music. But they ended up in the fields of deception, and they are not a nice place. Not at all. Think of what you felt in the forest times ten, with hallucinations on top."

Tori thought of the despair she'd felt in the gray mist. "That sounds awful. What did they see there?"

Malcolm explained. "Imagine every good dream you've ever had getting turned into a nightmare. Maybe you really wanted to win a hockey tournament, Hudson. Well, the fields of deception would show that to you, clear as day, and then it would twist into a different image. It would turn into you not just losing the tournament but getting kicked off the team, or breaking a leg, or something awful. Or it would show your best friend turning on you in betrayal. It is a nasty place that brings up all your deepest fears and twists your dreams around with them." He paused, looking sympathetically at the group sitting on the pastel cushions.

"But the only way through it is through it. Those poor children had to face all their biggest fears and keep going through each one. And the fields make it all look so real. It's hard to know what is real and what is a hallucination. The only thing that kept them going was wee John over there, that young pint-sized gnome. He helped them find the courage to face their fears. He may be small, but that's a mighty warrior. I'd hate to think what would have happened if they hadn't pushed through those illusions. They weren't real, of course, but fear is such a tricky thing. It can make everything seem so real. They could have been driven mad if they'd stayed in there too long."

They were silent for a moment, realizing how lucky they were that they all had made it here. Malcolm and Seamus had made the trip up the North Passage feel like an adventure, and they'd all persevered through the forest. But the truth was they were far from home and in a place of magic, and not all magic was kind and fluffy. Just like the world wasn't right now. What had happened at home with the earthquakes and tornadoes was every bit as scary as the fields of deception, and it was real.

They walked over quietly to the newest group of children to see if they could extend some much-needed hugs. As they did, the crystal cave's lighting began to change.

They looked up to see the cause. A disco ball like the one in the other cavern had dropped down from the top of the golden dome. It sent out a rainbow of soft lights that reflected on the walls. As the ball turned, the lights created a strobe effect, bouncing off the crystal wall, creating every color and pattern you could imagine. The six Weavers gathered in the center of the room, along with a few more who had just arrived.

Their clothing and looks were as varied as the rainbow of colors reflecting off the walls. But as they linked hands, creating a circle, they became perfectly harmonious. They started to rotate and dance in a circle, chanting in an unknown language, and the disco ball turned with them.

Seamus laughed under his breath, "I think we've officially arrived at the hippy convention."

Tori laughed, "But they are so cool. Look at how they're moving with the light. I think it's magical."

The children and gnomes stood outside the circle, watching the elves dance. The Weavers began to move faster, and the light also began to spin faster. Their chanting picked up in speed, the words blurring together. Soon, they were moving so fast you couldn't tell them apart, moving faster than any human could move. They started to lift off the ground, a whirling circle of color and movement.

The intensity picked up, and the children stared in awe. An electricity filled the air, building like a charge in the room. The circle began to shrink as the Weavers and the lights started to move closer together. The disco ball began to shine into the center of the room, sending down a beam of swirling rainbow light. The Weavers moved closer and closer together, merging into the beam.

"How is this even possible?" Tori said out loud. It looked like they were quite literally turning into one being. The movement was so fast it looked like it wasn't moving at all. The electricity and energy created made Hudson's hair stand up on his arms. The light intensified, every color of the rainbow coming into one stream of white light. And then.

Bam.

The Weavers disappeared in a flash of light and silence.

Where the Weavers had been now stood a large wooden loom, a machine used to weave carpets and tapestries. It looked ancient, the wood dark and worn. On the loom was a long tapestry, partly finished. Many threads were feeding into the front, and the woven tapestry was coming out the back. There was a chair sitting in front of it, but no elves.

The children and gnomes gathered around the loom, looking at the long length of intricately woven tapestry neatly stacked and folded. One child lifted it and looked under it, wondering if the elves were hiding underneath, but no, there was no one.

Where had they gone?

* * *

Thirteen

Finding Your Thread

The children continued to examine the weaving loom, while a few gnomes went to look for the Weavers. Tori and Hudson picked up the tapestry with the help of three other children and laid it out so they could see its full length. It was the most curious design, full of different colors and textures of thread. In one sense, it didn't seem to have any pattern at all. There were no real shapes or designs, but it had bands of color that varied in thickness. There was a long part that was mostly green, with different shades of green woven in, and a few bright gold and silver threads popping out. Then it shifted to a brown band, which was shorter, then a black section.

The black area was dark and bleak, with only a few gold threads. Then the gold threads increased, and the next stretch of the tapestry was almost all gold. Then it changed colors to blue.

Hudson took a closer look at the gold and blue section.

"Look, Tori, even in this blue you can see all the other colors inside. There are red and green threads, but they come together and still look like blue. How weird. I wonder what it's for? I don't think I'd like a rug that looks like this on my floor."

They had a large woven rug at home with interlacing circles and triangles in gray and blue. It was a nice pattern. This rug, or whatever it was, didn't look like it should be going in someone's living room.

"Over here!" a boy called to the group. He was looking at the front of the loom, where the yarn was fed into the machine. "Look at these baskets." The baskets were filled with different balls of yarn, and they were every color and shade you could imagine. There was copper yarn, pearl yarn, and purple yarn. There was rainbow colored yarn, and yarn that was so bright it looked like sunshine. There was yarn that was so black it sucked the light from your eyes. Tori picked up some of the different yarns, feeling the texture. The pearl-colored yarn was soft and slippery, and the sunshine yarn was warm to the touch. The black yarn burned her hand.

"Ouch!" She dropped it back into the basket. "Since when does yarn burn your hand?"

A tall girl peered at the front of the loom, pointing to several thicker strings that were coming out of the front, and were perpendicular to the rest of the yarn.

"What are those?" she asked.

Just as she asked, one of the gnomes returned, with a very tall Weaver by his side.

"Good question!" He replied. "Good question indeed! Let's see if I can answer that for you."

"And what happened to the other Weavers?" another child asked.

The elf laughed, "Ah, yes, so many questions. Children are always good for that, aren't they? Not afraid to ask questions. Well, good, good, the more questions the better, though the answers may not always leave you satisfied. Come, let's all sit down, and I will explain."

The children crowded around the tall elf, who was twice the height of the gnomes and taller than most of the children.

He had a long, gray beard and gray robes. He walked with a staff, but stood strong and straight. It looked more like a wizard's staff than a cane, though he did appear to be quite old. His face was pale and wrinkled, and his eyes were a unique gray color. They looked like the gray of a dark storm cloud with flecks of blue and green.

He sat down in the chair in front of the loom and motioned for the children to sit on the floor around him. Cushions magically flew over to the group, placing themselves just as each child sat down. When all were settled, the elf looked kindly at the group.

"Now, dear ones, let us start with the first question."

He pointed to the thick strings coming out of the loom. "These are called warp threads. You might say they are what gives the shape of the tapestry." He pointed to the long fabric coming out of the back. "They guide the threads that are woven in between. Those are called the weft. The weft threads give the tapestry color, texture, and pattern."

He pointed to six of the guiding threads, or warps. "As for your second question, my fellow Weavers are here. These six lovely warp threads right here. Along with some other Weavers you hadn't met yet."

There was a sharp intake of breath as the children heard the Weavers had turned into a thread. "Oh, don't worry, your new friends didn't change into a string never to be seen again. They are just taking on a different form for now, so you can see what's normally hidden. You see, my young friends, this is the Tapestry of Life." He pointed to the long tapestry that stretched out behind the loom, extending almost to the edge of the cavern. "Each living being is part of its story. All of you are threads in this beautiful tapestry, as were your parents and grandparents before them. As are the gnomes and all the elves. And the Weavers, well, we are the warp threads. We create the framework of the story, because we ARE the framework."

Tori stared at the elf, confused. "Yes, I know it's all a bit warped," he laughed at his own pun. "But you have to remember we are in the Crystal Cave of Contemplation at the North Pole. I'm sure you've noticed that things are quite a bit different here than in your home. Gravity, magic, and even what you can see with your eyes. I am here speaking to you, while also in this loom as one of the longest warp threads in the tapestry. It is only your eyes that are making it feel confusing. Reality is more than what you see. There is so much going on in that space beyond our sight."

The old elf paused, seeing he had lost the kids back at his own joke about warp threads and warped realities.

"Perhaps I should start at the beginning." The gnomes all nodded in unison, and the children smiled. He adjusted his robes, settled into the chair, and began his story.

"All good stories seem to begin with once upon a time. Let's begin that way, too." He paused and smiled softly.

"Once upon a time, a group of elves discovered some crystal caves. They were fascinated by the caves and began to explore them. While they explored, they noticed that the crystals affected their minds. Nothing dangerous or anything, but they seemed to open up parts of their brains that had been asleep. They began to see colors more vividly, and smell and taste more intensely. Their senses became heightened. So naturally, they wanted to spend more time in the caves! They would come here to sing, dance, and cook their meals because all of those experiences were more joyful and delightful in the caves. Dancing was a favorite pastime, as the crystals seemed to light up when they danced. But their senses also became heightened in other ways, especially when they were still. When they sat quietly in the caves, they began to see and hear things that were beyond what eyes and ears could see and hear. You might say it was 'extra-sensory.' I would say that it was always there, but they hadn't learned to see it yet. And that was the real magic of these caves."

He paused to look at all the children who sat in rapt attention. Settling deeper into his chair, he continued. "The caves helped the elves begin to see that all of life was connected. And that each living being was a thread, connecting with other threads, like the threads in a tapestry. The more time they spent in the caves, the more the caves taught them. And the more they learned, the less they wanted to leave. And that is when we began to think of ourselves as the Weavers, because we could see the weave of the world."

The old elf's eyes lit up. "I tell you it is the most beautiful thing! The way we began to flow within it was like a whole other kind of dance. Did you enjoy Clyde's music earlier? He was just playing the music of the weave. The sounds of the sea and the forest."

He looked up at the crystal ceiling, giving it a curious look. "But the crystals weren't done with us yet. We don't know exactly what it is about this area on the Earth, or this particular cave, but it seems to be the center of the story of the world. What is the story of the world, you may ask?" He turned to the loom and pointed to the tapestry.

"That, my friends, is the story of the world. We used a bit of magic to turn it into a form you can see, but the story is there, even if you can't touch it with your hands or see it with your eyes. And the crystals showed us that the Weavers played a bigger part in that story than we had ever guessed. It showed us we are the guides, quite literally, that shape the story itself."

The elf gently touched one of the threads that he had called the warp. "This one is me. You may be wondering how I can be there and at the same time talking to you? The same way that the other Weavers were talking to you before, and are now gone. They are the other warp threads." He touched the one next to his. "This is Clyde, and this one is Jasmine," he said, touching a third thread.

"Let me explain. The tapestry in front of you is a magical construct we created for you. That's what the elves were doing in their dance, creating a bit of magic so you could see the tapestry and understand the story of the world. You can't see the actual tapestry with your eyes, only with the vision beyond vision. And since you haven't been training in the caves for hundreds of years to get that sight, this is a pretty good replica."

"Umm, excuse me, Mister Weaver Elf," a young girl spoke up.

He turned to look at her. "Forgive me, please call me Merlin. What is your question, dear Lucy?" He smiled warmly, somehow knowing her name without her ever saying.

"Well," she continued, "it seems like you are very important elves, but your threads are boring gray. All the others are different colors. Why aren't yours?"

"Ah, yes," he answered. "I did say we play an important part in the story of the world, but not all the big parts in a story are the ones you know about. Think about a play. There are all the actors you see on stage, but what about all the people you don't see? The set makers, the directors, the lighting and sound people, and the people who sell the tickets. There are so many parts to a story, but not all are bright and shiny. The weft threads create the shape of a tapestry but not the design itself. You'll never see them in a finished weaving. Just like that, the Weavers create the shape of the story and guide it through its different stages, but we don't write the story itself. That is what all of you do. While we are the warp threads, each of you are the weft threads."

He points to the colorful threads feeding into the front of the loom. "These are your threads, children. Yours and everyone else alive in this world. You are the ones creating the story. We only give you the scenes, set, and backdrops."

Hudson had been listening intently and began to understand what

142

Merlin was saying. He asked a question. "Is that why there are different blocks of color on the tapestry? Like, sometimes it's all green for a while, and then sometimes it's all blue? Are you setting different scenes?"

Merlin turned to him and smiled. "Yes, Hudson, exactly so." He stood up and walked to the back of the loom. "See here," he picked up the green stretch. "This was a time when humans were closely connected to nature. There was a lot of rain, the plants grew well, and everyone thrived." Then he pointed to the brown part below it. "Here, the rains dried up, and many plants died. It was a harder time, but look here, how many gold threads started to appear. These were the humans who found ways to conserve water or change farming practices. They were innovators and helped many people."

Now Tori had a question. "Excuse me, Merlin, but if you are part of the group who is guiding this story, why would you make times when people didn't have enough food to eat? Or why would you make a time like now? With earthquakes and people dying? Or wars?"

Other children began to nod in agreement. If these elves were shaping this tapestry, why wouldn't they make it happy and peaceful?

Merlin nodded slowly. "That is a very good question, but I have to explain something first. While we are these warp threads, we don't decide where we go in the tapestry or what shape it takes. We are just aware of the shape before it happens. We can see the future, or at least the shape of it, but we can't change it."

Tori nodded, feeling a bit more at ease that the elves weren't intentionally creating wars.

"But, to answer your bigger question. Why do we have wars and droughts? Why not have things be joyful and peaceful? I can't truly answer why, but I can tell you that all of life is in cycles, and always will be. Look at the weather. We have four seasons, and each year plants start off growing in the spring. In the summer, they produce fruit. In the autumn, the plants are harvested, and things die back. In the winter, the plants go to sleep. Then the next year it starts all over again. That story is the same, but in the tapestry of life, it happens on a much larger scale. There are ages of growth, like the spring. There are ages of joy and abundance, like summer and fall. There are ages of hardship, like the winter. Things get old and must die to be reborn into something new. These are the different color blocks you see on the tapestry."

The children nodded slowly, letting the idea sink into their brains.

Tori still wasn't sure how she felt, but living on a farm, she could understand the concept. Things were hard for the animals in the winter. They had to heat the water troughs to keep them from freezing, and they often lost an older animal during the winter. In the Spring, the goats would have kids, the chickens would hatch chicks, and it felt cheerful and hopeful.

She started to think about her history lessons, talking about the Egyptians, then the Romans, then the Dark Ages, and then the Renaissance. Were these the same Ages as what was on the Tapestry? Like the seasons, but on a bigger scale?

Merlin continued, almost as if reading Tori's mind. "There are smaller cycles and bigger cycles and even bigger cycles in the Tapestry. One year is a small cycle. A bigger cycle is a generation of humans. Each generation is a little bit different. Then there are the Ages. This is the Age of the Egyptians, when they were the keepers of the wisdom of the world." He pointed to a part of the tapestry that had colors very much like an Egyptian painting: reds, oranges, browns, and golds. "Here is the Dark Ages. There was a lot of fighting because the wisdom had been lost after the downfall of the Roman civilization." The Dark Ages were dull and gray, but in between them were also a lot of blue and green. "Look here, the dark ages weren't all bad, despite what your history books say. There was a beautiful connection to earth and water here. See these beautiful aquamarine threads?" He pointed out blue threads in the gray.

"And then, even bigger than Ages are Epochs. Epochs are very long cycles, and so the shifting of them can feel quite big. Did you ever hear about the people of Atlantis? Their great cities that were lost to the sea? That was the end of an Epoch." He pointed far back in the tapestry. The colors and textures of that part of the tapestry had a completely different texture. The threads were all shiny and slippery-looking, like they were coated in something.

"Children, the reason we brought you here. The reason I'm telling you this story is that is where we are now. The end of an Epoch. That is what all the earthquakes and storms were. The Earth is getting ready for a major shift. It will be as big as the one back then. The whole texture and shape of the Tapestry is about to change." He paused. "Completely."

"And you, each of you, are going to be the threads that write that new story."

Everyone's eyes widened.

"Come, children, stand next to me and look closely at the tapestry."

The children crowded around Merlin. He walked them to the long tapestry coming out of the back of the loom. He brought them back to the last Epoch, where he said was the end of Atlantis, and where all the threads were of a different texture. They looked at the different ages since then. There were many colors, but all the threads looked like cotton or wool. Then he showed them the threads at the front of the loom. The ones being woven right now. Many of them were dark gray, some even black. Many of the threads were rough, as if made of the roughest wool. But in between them were pearly-looking threads. Those threads were gold, silver, and a pearly blues.

The elf looked at a young boy, probably about nine. "So Dominic, which thread would you like to be?"

"I get to choose?" Dominic asked.

Merlin laughed, "Of course! You always get to choose!"

"I want to be one of the gold ones!" He pointed down at the basket with gold thread.

"Great choice," Merlin said. "Now to be that thread means next year when you try out for football, you're going to have to accept that captain position they offer you."

Dominic looked terrified, "But I can't be captain. That's way too big a responsibility. What if they don't like me?"

Merlin had hit a nerve. "Ah, yes, that is the thing about the gold thread. You have to face your fears of not being liked and go out and do it anyway." Dominic nodded solemnly, understanding what the elf meant.

He turned to Tori, "What color thread would you like to be?"

She looked carefully in the basket. She didn't want to be a bright, shiny thread. Her favorite things in life were hanging out and laughing with friends, and helping out at the rink cafe. She saw a pink-purple thread. She picked it up, and it was the softest material. It felt like a big hug, and the pink and purple swirled together, multiple threads creating a thick yarn. "I like this one."

Merlin smiled, "Yes, that is an important one. Threads of kindness and love to weave into the story. These dark gray and black threads need that more than ever, to brighten up the picture."

"Whose threads are those?" she asked. "They look very sad."

"That is exactly right, my dear. There is a lot of sadness and fear right now, and it makes people feel hopeless. They are creating a very dark weave. Very dark indeed. So dark, I think that is why it was time for a system reset."

Hudson looked quietly at the tapestry and the baskets.

"I don't know what color I want to be yet," he said. "I kind of like all the colors."

Merlin nodded knowingly. "Me too young man, me too. And that is the beauty of life. You don't have to be one color for your whole life. You get to choose, and you will choose, whether you see this tapestry or not. Every time you make a choice in life, you are choosing one of the colors of thread. Every time you pick fear or love, you are picking a color. Every time you pick kindness, or silliness, or laughter, you are choosing your color. Or when you are serious and sit down and do homework instead of playing a game, you are picking a color. The warp threads set the shape of the story, but all of you are the weft. You create the tale. Your destiny is in every choice you make."

Hudson wasn't so sure about that answer. "But what if I make the wrong choice?"

Merlin laughed, realizing he'd frightened him. "Well then, you just make a different choice the next time. Don't worry, there are no wrong choices. The whole world is a tapestry of different colors and textures. All of them were made of billions and trillions of choices, but none of them were wrong. They were just part of the story. But, of course, I do like stories with a few good jokes in them, don't you?"

Hudson laughed in agreement, "For sure. Those stories are way better."

Merlin's eyes swept across the group. "All of you are here today, at this moment, because you are supposed to be here." His voice turned serious. "We, the Weavers, knew this change in Epochs was coming, and created that prophecy ages ago to prepare for this moment. But the prophecy ends here. Not because the world is ending, but because we don't know what comes next. The change is that big."

A small girl next to him widened her eyes in concern.

"But don't be afraid. Change is not something to be afraid of. It is as natural as the seasons." He put his hand on her shoulder. "And you, the children of this world, are the ones who will help us with this change.

You will guide us into that new Epoch."

He walked over to the loom and picked up one of the pearlescent threads. "You are so special. You are made of a new texture of thread, and bring new colors not yet seen in the Tapestry of Life. Most of the adults on this planet are made of the old textures and the old ways. People may call you out as different. But that's because you are! We could almost say you are mutations, though that's a funny word. Maybe it would be better to say you are evolving."

He put the thread down and looked at each of them in turn before continuing, "You saw how the threads of the old Epoch, the days of Atlantis, looked slippery. You saw how the threads of this Epoch are cotton or wool. Notice how many of the threads in this basket are soft and shiny. You are the threads in this basket. You haven't been a big part of the tapestry yet, but you are coming into it now. You are different, and that's precisely the point! That is why you are the ones who will lead us into the new world."

Merlin started to get excited, waving his hands up into the air as he spoke. "Don't you see children? You think about things differently from the adults. You see things differently. You feel differently. Don't be afraid of this! All these dark threads are afraid of your differences. They are afraid of change. But you can't help who you are, so don't try. You are exactly who you are meant to be, and you are being born in the exact moment you are meant to be born in. You are meant to be these new threads in the basket."

"You are going to make a whole new weave! And let me tell you children, I think it is going to be absolutely beautiful." His passion and enthusiasm for this change were pouring out of his voice.

"I know, it won't be easy. And I know that there have been a lot of hard things going on right now. But if you could see it the way I saw it, with as long as I've been a part of this loom? Well, all I can say is this is a really exciting time. Really exciting."

Malcolm, who'd been quiet in the back, came forward and looked into the baskets of threads. Then he looked at the dark, rough threads on the loom.

"I'm with you, Merlin!" He cried out enthusiastically. "I'm ready to see some of those new threads on the tapestry. If a reset is needed to make that happen, I say bring it on!"

The gnomes hurrahed in agreement, though the children were not quite so enthusiastic. Hudson thought of all the damage that had been done to the house, the farm, and the roads around him.

Merlin could sense their concern and said to them, "Truly, children, I understand. Who would want to be born into a time of so much change and hardship? But I have been in this cave for longer than you can imagine. I have been a part of the Tapestry for so many lifetimes. Even when it doesn't feel like it, everything is unfolding as it's meant to. You are here because you are the ones who bring that new color into the world. When things start to feel dark or scary, remember that. Have faith in the story even if you lose faith in yourself. The shape is already there. It is just for you to fill in the details."

Hudson let out a big sigh. It felt like a big responsibility, but it also felt pretty cool that they were asking the kids, and not adults, to write the story of the world.

"So, what do you say, kids?" Merlin grinned knowingly. "Shall we reset the system? Shall we create a new Epoch?"

* * *

Fourteen

Resetting the System

Merlin directed the kids to step back from the loom. "I need space for this next bit of magic."

The children and gnomes moved back towards the seating areas. "Excellent," Merlin directed. "Now go ahead and create a circle, gnomes and humans all together." They complied. "Great. You look fantastic. Now, look to your left and right." The children all turned. Tori was standing by Hudson and Seamus.

"If you know them," he continued, "go stand next to someone else. Go and make friends with a stranger. Say hello. Don't worry. We're all friends here."

Tori and Hudson moved around the circle to stand next to children they hadn't met. Tori ended up next to a young girl from Korea and a boy from South Africa. They introduced themselves, smiling and shaking hands. Hudson ended up next to a boy from Sydney, Australia, and a gnome from Germany. They shook hands.

"Okay, now that you've all met, hold hands to make a circle." The children and the gnomes took each other's hands while Merlin stood in the center.

"You remember I said the loom was a bit of a magical illusion? To help you see what was already there but couldn't see? To reset the system, I'll need to send the loom back into the dreamscape and bring back our Weaver friends. All you need to do is stand together and hold the space for me."

The disco ball at the top of the ceiling lit up as he spoke and started to swirl rainbow colors on the walls of the cave. Merlin lifted his hands into the air and started to mumble words quietly. He paused for a moment and looked at them. "Oh yeah, and one thing, don't forget to smile. Happiness makes everything go better." The children laughed a bit and smiled.

The disco ball light concentrated down onto the loom, the rainbow swirls focusing like a beam. The ball began to rotate very fast. As it did, the light started to dissolve different parts of the loom. First, the chair disappeared, then the feet of the loom broke up and dissolved into the light. The light moved up like a laser beam, dissolving more and more of the loom until it got to the part where the tapestry was. It focused on that area, and the light became very intense. It was so bright it was painful to look at, and most of the kids closed their eyes. Hudson kept his eyes open for a bit longer and saw the loom dissolve into one tiny pinpoint of light, almost as bright as the sun. He squinted so the light wouldn't hurt his eyes, but kept watching.

Then the pinpoint of light turned itself inside out. It was like turning a bag inside out to reveal what was inside. Out of that pinpoint of light came all the Weaver elves. They grew from the size of a piece of sand to a full-sized elf in seconds. The intense light faded away, and the disco ball stopped turning. The loom was gone, and in its place were the Weavers looking at the children with contented smiles.

"Well done, well done," Merlin beamed, bowing to the children and clapping his hands.

"So, that was the easy part. Now, here's where it gets fun. To reset the system, we reset the warp threads. We're going to weave a new story into the tapestry. And you're going to help us!"

The Weavers created a circle within the circle of children and gnomes. There were 13 of them, including Merlin. They reached out to hold hands, and as soon as the last two hands connected, a hum began to fill the room. Tori looked around, trying to see where the sound came from. It wasn't the Weavers. They were quiet, though they had started to sway in rhythm to the humming. The hum was coming from the cave itself. She whispered quietly, "Are the crystals singing?"

The girl next to her nodded, looking around at the cave walls.

Merlin spoke loudly, voice booming out into the room. "Once an Epoch, we are given a chance to change the story of the world. Once an Epoch change comes so great that the very texture of reality can shift into a new way of being. Dearest children, we are at one of those moments. The story of the world is ready for a new chapter, and you are here to write it. Help us create the warps for that story, so that you may be the wefts to weave in the details. What shall the shape of that tapestry become?"

Hudson was thinking about the actual tapestry they'd been looking at, and was confused about what Merlin meant. He asked tentatively, "What do you mean, what shape will it be? Isn't it a rectangle?"

Merlin smiled kindly at him, appreciating his courage for asking the question. "Ah yes, Hudson, you are still thinking with your mind. It is time to think with your heart. Close your eyes, children, and feel your hearts. Ask them the question, what does the story of the world want to look like? What texture shall we put into the tapestry?"

The humming of the crystal cave grew louder, and the disco ball began to turn again, sending every color imaginable around the room, shining onto the children.

Tori closed her eyes and imagined how she would want the world to be different. "I want good people to run the government," she said. "And that there is no more cancer."

Merlin smiled, "Beautiful Tori. Thank you. Let us create a warp thread of healing and one for wise leaders."

The Weavers began to rotate in their circle, swaying to the musical hum of the crystals.

A young girl called out, "I want the ground to be filled with trampolines instead of grass, and all the trees are soft like marshmallows."

Merlin laughed, "That sounds like great fun, Mila! We will build a lighter, bouncier, and softer world into the weave."

The light responded to his words, sending green and blue light down towards the circle.

Hudson called out, "I want people not to murder each other."

The disco ball light intensified as he spoke, sending a golden beam of light into the space inside the Weavers' circle.

Another child spoke up quietly, "I want people not to feel lonely and commit suicide."

Pink light shone down from the disco ball, wrapping them all in a soft glow. Other children spoke up, sharing their dreams for what the world could look like.

"I want every day to feel like Christmas!" a child said gleefully, remembering they were at the North Pole.

"I wish there were no more bullies and people were nice to each other," said another.

"I hope that all the homeless people have homes and all the cats and dogs are adopted."

"I want school to be outside in the forest and not inside memorizing boring facts."

Merlin nodded at each addition, directing the messages into the warp threads.

The Weavers swayed and danced in their circle, the crystal cave humming a beautiful melody. The melody and the light responded to the words of the children, changing color and tune with each addition.

The children, holding hands, also began to sway back and forth to the sound. A feeling of love and joy was growing in the room. It spread from heart to heart of each child, gnome, and elf. Each felt as if they were creating a new world, right then and there, as their words shaped the Tapestry of Life.

Merlin spoke as if in a trance

> *And so it is, and so it shall be.*
> *The words become the reality.*
> *The warp is set, the weft to come,*
> *A new Epoch has begun.*

The Weavers joined him in chanting the words. "And so it is, and so it shall be. The words become the reality. The warp is set, the weft to come, a new Epoch has begun."

The disco ball began to slow and then stop. The humming stopped. The walls of the crystal cave glowed a luminous gold color as the children, gnomes, and Weavers stood in silence.

Tori began to feel a shift in the room, though at first, she wasn't sure what it was. The air smelled different, like the smell of a fresh spring day. It smelled like a day when the sun is warm but not hot, and cherry blossom petals fall from the trees, drifting in the sky. The light in the room looked different, too. It had gone from a bright swirling dance party to the warm glow of a sunrise. But there was a pearly quality to the air she'd never seen before, as if the air itself had a shimmer to it.

But more than that, there was a shift in the energy in the room. She could feel it, almost like electricity in the air before a storm. It made her skin tingle, but not in a scary way. It tingled with what felt like hope and possibility.

Malcolm looked around in awe. As a magical being, he could see things that humans couldn't. And he could sense the shift in the story of the world. He could almost see how the air had changed chemistry. Something was different, and it would never be the same again.

Merlin dropped his hands, and the other Weavers followed suit. They stood back and turned to look at the children. They smiled, their eyes full of love.

Merlin bowed to the children, his eyes full of humility. "Thank you, dear ones. Thank you for your warmth, your love, and your hope. We have reset the system. And it is beautiful to behold."

The children also dropped their hands, and Tori and Hudson went to find Seamus and Malcolm. Tori wrapped them all in a big hug, her heart full of love and warmth. Hudson also hugged the gnomes, his heart full of peace and joy.

But then he returned to his sillier side. "That was wild," he exclaimed. "Did you feel that? And the lights? Weren't they crazy?"

Malcolm nodded and grinned. "It was indeed! I don't know about you, but I'm famished from all that seriousness. Hey, Merlin," he called out to the old elf. "What's a gnome got to do to get some tea and cake around here?"

Merlin laughed loudly, and the mood lifted. The light in the cave responded accordingly and returned to a cheerful yellow. The Weavers guided the children back to the tie-dye cushions and managed to pull, pretty much out of thin air, a feast of tea, cakes, cookies, and other delights.

Before long, the kids were laughing and carrying on, tossing tiny cushions at each other. Clyde was playing his magic flute in the corner, floating a few feet above the ground, and the elves and gnomes told each other stories over tea and cake.

Merlin stood back from the group, with a quiet smile, looking happily at the scene.

* * *

The North Passage

***

Fifteen

Returning Home

After everyone had eaten, the elves whisked away the plates and cups. Merlin had disappeared. A tall elf with long blond hair told Hudson that he often wandered away. "He seems to only show up when there's some action to be had, and then he goes off back into the caves," she laughed. "I'm the one who keeps us organized and fed around here."

She spoke up to the group, "Dear ones, thank you for your courage and fearlessness. For leaving your homes, for traveling the underground rivers, and for finding your way to these caves that few have ever seen. Maybe it is your youth that lets you do things that feel impossible to the old, because no one else has managed to find their way here in a very long time!"

Hudson grinned, feeling quite proud of himself.

She continued, "You said yes to adventure, and yes to the unknown. And because you did, we are ready to start a new chapter in the story of the world."

She pulled out a bag with letters in it. "These are letters from Merlin to each of you. He asked you not to read them until you are back safely home. He wanted to remind you that just because we had this amazing experience today, the work is not over."

She gestured to the Weavers standing around her. "You helped us set the warp threads. But those threads only create the shape of the story. You are the ones who will create the weave. You are the ones who pick the color, the texture, and the pattern. It will be every day, by the choices you make or don't make, and the courage to choose love and adventure over fear. You are the ones who create the story. We just hold the space for you." She smiled warmly at them, dipping her head in a bow.

"Safe travels home, and I hope your passage back is less challenging than it was here." She paused. "And I hope you return to find some things having shifted for the better. It was a dark time indeed when you left your homes."

She looked at all the gnomes now. "And thank you, cousins and friends. For protecting and guiding these beautiful and brave spirits on their adventures. I am sure you will always keep an eye on them, even after this journey is finished."

Seamus, who had been very quiet during his time in the caves, now spoke up. "Ay, that's for sure, lassie. These wee children will always have friends with the gnomes. They are a beautiful and brave lot, to be sure."

Tori smiled appreciatively and reached out to Seamus, giving him a warm hug.

Then Malcolm spoke up, "And thank you, dear cousins, for your hospitality and all that you do for the world. It must get lonely here at times. If you ever feel like a change of scene, may I extend an open invitation to visit, on behalf of all gnomes?" The other gnomes nodded enthusiastically.

He then continued, looking at Tori and Hudson, "Well, I guess if we are to be going, better to do it now on a nice full tummy, than wait until we're hungry again!"

Hudson laughed but agreed. "And I want to get back home to see all my animals! I miss them!"

Tori added, "And our parents, too, Hudson."

Hudson looked a little embarrassed to have thought about his animals before his parents. "Oh yes, of course. Them too."

The elves handed out the letters to all the children, and the gnomes filled bags with food and provisions for the journey home.

Hudson hugged his new friend Chetan goodbye, realizing he'd probably never see him again. He hoped he would find things a little better when they got home. Then he found Seamus and Malcolm.

"Malcolm," Hudson asked, "do we have to go through that awful forest again?"

"Good question. Let me see," he replied, and walked over to one of the Weavers.

"Say now, there must be an easier way to get out of here than the way we came?"

The Weaver looked at the kids who still had scraped knees, "Oh yes, yes of course! That was just the magic needed to get you here. You'll find the main path back to the North Pole Village as sunny and straightforward as can be."

"So, no fields of deception?" a child asked, hearing the conversation.

"Yes, quite right. I mean, the fields will still be there, but the deception part will be gone. It was there to keep people out of the caves. It won't affect you on the way back," the elf replied. "You'll be perfectly safe."

"I hope so," mumbled Hudson. "I don't want to look like those kids did when they walked in."

The elf insisted the fields would be sunny and clear, and the path would be visible. "Of course, you still have to take the rivers home, and I can't control what happens once you leave the North Pole. But here you are protected."

She guided them to the exit of the cave. "Travel well, my friends, travel well." Then she added mysteriously, "And we will see you in the Tapestry."

The gnomes and children walked out of the cave into bright and snowy sunshine. The crystal cave and all its mystery faded away as they looked at snow-covered pine trees and a well-marked path stretching out in front of them. The air was crisp and cold, and the cavern ceiling was filled with sunshine and fluffy clouds floating along.

As they walked along the path, they came upon a field that was empty of trees or plants, but also of any other images or hallucinations. "This is where we saw all those horrible things," a little boy whispered to Hudson.

Hudson put a reassuring hand on the boy's arm. "They're gone now. See?" He pointed to the empty fields. "It was just imagination."

The boy shivered slightly, still struggling to shake off his experience.

They passed through the fields and, as they went up over a hill, could see the village of the North Pole below.

"Look!" Tori exclaimed, "We're almost there!"

"To the village, yes," Seamus replied amusedly. "But don't forget, lassie, we still have the North Passage to go through. And then, well, who knows what we will find at home."

Tori looked down, "Oh yeah, I forgot."

Seamus continued, "And we best keep going. No need to sit around eating candy with the elves. We've got homes to return to!"

Tori suddenly realized Seamus had a home too, though he didn't often talk about it. "Was your home damaged by the earthquakes?" She asked him.

"My home?" he replied. "Yes and no. I spend most of my time on my boat. But I do sometimes go back to my sister's house, or to visit Malcolm. My sister's house collapsed, and her family is staying with a neighbor. I want to get home to her and make sure she's okay and help out a bit. Now that our parents are gone, we've only got each other."

"I had no idea you had a sister or that you lost your parents," Tori exclaimed. "I'm so sorry."

"Aww, it's alright, my dear," Seamus said sheepishly. "I don't talk much about myself. It's just my nature. But I appreciate your caring." He looked ahead to the village to change the subject.

"Look up there!" he exclaimed, pointing to the lake. "The elves are already gathered around our boats. They must have known we were coming."

The group walked through the village and out to the lake, meeting a large group of elves waiting for them. They erupted in a great round of applause and cheers as the children arrived.

"You did it!" Jaquin cried out. "Well done! Well done! We can feel the shift already."

"You can?" Tori asked. "How?"

He explained. "Well, we're magical creatures, of course, much more sensitive than humans. We all sensed a change in the air an hour ago. It was like a new breeze, fresh and clear, came through on the wind."

Tori was amazed because that was how it felt to her in the crystal caves.

"Yes, exactly," another added. "We don't know where that wind is going to take you, but it feels so much lighter than the air before."

A girl called out, "Lighter, like the ground is made of trampolines?"

"Indeed!" Jaquin laughed, "Quite possibly! Who knows what the future holds with you at the helm?"

Seamus exclaimed, "I'm happy to have these young ones in charge. They seem a lot more fun than those old grumps currently running the show!" They all laughed, and the elves walked with them to their boats.

Boats of every color, shape, and size lined the edge of the lake. They were as varied as the children who had come in them. Some were long and low in the water, others were tall and narrow, with sailing masts. Some had figures of dragons etched on the side, and others had pictures of mermaids and dolphins. The children said their goodbyes and got into their boats, ready to make their journey back home.

Tori and Hudson felt more hopeful than when they arrived. But as the boat pushed off the sandy shore, they still felt worry and anxiety about returning home. What would they find?

"Do you think they've had any more earthquakes at home?" Hudson asked.

Tori replied, "I don't think so. Or we would have felt them here. Or someone would have said. The elves said they could feel a good shift in the air. I hope that's true."

Seamus guided the boat through the smooth lake and towards the passage that would take them back to the North Passage.

The water was clear and calm, reflecting the clouds above in its tranquil waters.

"Enjoy it while it lasts," Seamus called to them. "Did I forget to mention that all water runs downhill? In other words, the rivers travel faster south than they do north."

"Seamus, what are you talking about?" Hudson asked. "Rivers can't flow in two directions!"

"And elves can't live underground," Seamus laughed. "And there's no such thing as the North Pole. Don't always believe everything you hear. And besides, things work differently down here. How else do you think I'd get around without a sail? The water flows where it needs to go, it doesn't matter what direction we go in."

Hudson shook his head again. For some reason, he could accept everything he'd seen and experienced over the last week, but water flowing two ways was too much for him.

"I'll see it when I believe it," he finally said.

"Ay, that you will, laddie, that you will."

Seamus guided them out of the large cave and into a side tunnel that looked familiar. It was the tunnel they'd sailed through days before when they'd come to the North Pole. Tori let out a happy sigh. They were going home. But as soon as they entered the tunnel, the water began to pick up, moving them ahead.

Seamus was right. This was the same river that had propelled them to the North Pole, but now the current was taking them away.

"Huh," Hudson said, staring at the river. "Weird."

Tori grinned, "Only if you say so, Hudson. I think it's kinda cool."

Malcolm laughed, "Magic's always good for turning gravity on its head every now and again."

The stream began to pick up, and the tunnel widened. Seamus steered them around two or three bends, and then he said, "Okay, kids, buckle up and sit tight. We're about to go back into the North Passage. And like the Fields of Deception were gone, I think the Veil of Illusion will be too. I don't think there's going to be anything holding us back from full speed ahead."

"Are you ready?" Malcolm chimed in.

"We're ready!" Tori cried out, locking her fingers onto the side of the boat and sitting down in her chair. "Will we need the oars to help steer?"

"Not yet," Seamus said. "For now, I think it will just be fast and furious."

Seamus wasn't exaggerating. As he steered them through the mouth of the tunnel back to the main river, the boat practically whipped around sideways into the fast-flowing current.

He stood tall in the back with his rudder in the water, steering the boat around rocks. But the water flowed so fast that even he couldn't control it much.

They rocketed down the river, the walls of the tunnel whizzing past them. They were moving so fast that Hudson's hair was flying back behind him. "It's like a supersonic speedway!" he called out, exhilarated by the pace.

The water roared through the tunnel, and yet there were no rapids or boulders at the moment, just a fast flow that led the boat straight through.

"We're going to be home in like five minutes at this rate!" Tori exclaimed.

"Not quite," Malcolm replied, keeping an eye out ahead for any danger, "But by night time to be sure!"

Given that it had taken them almost two days to get there, Hudson figured they must have been going twice as fast now. Seamus called out, "Duck and cover!"

The kids bent down to their knees, and the boat raced through a low point in the tunnel, the water propelling them even faster. The wood began to creak a bit from the strain of so much water pressing on their sides.

Seamus could hear the wood and assured the kids, "Not to worry. Ol' Bessie's been through this much and more. She'll be just fine. But I think we may need to get those oars out again."

The children sat back up again, found the oars, and got them ready to help Seamus steer.

"Now you remember what to do, right? When I say left, go left. When I say pull, pull. And when I say reverse, dig in hard and reverse." He called out to Malcolm, "Look lively, lad, I think the river's going to give us something to remember her by."

As if the river had a mind of its own, a wave splashed them suddenly, soaking Tori and Hudson.

Seamus chuckled as the kids pulled their wet hair from their faces. "Aww, just a little parting gift from the Mistress."

He looked ahead, and Malcolm raised his left hand.

"Pull left, kids!" he called out, "Quickly now."

They dug their oars hard to the left, as they skirted a huge boulder.

"Excellent, Excellent. Now, steady forward. Go. Go. Okay, now REVERSE!" he called out. "Give it all you got!"

They pulled hard, turning the boat sideways, just in time to escape a whirlpool that had appeared out of nowhere. "Okay, right now, right, quickly!"

They pulled hard to the right, flipping back around to face straight. The boat raced forward.

"Where did that come from?" Malcolm called back to the captain.

"Oh, you know, the river's always got a few tricks up her sleeve," Seamus replied. "Okay, children, steady on. Well done. We should be good for a moment or two."

The kids exhaled, but before they could properly relax, Seamus had their oars back in the water, navigating boulders and rapids.

The pace was so fast they didn't have time to think, just responding automatically to Seamus' orders. They were completely soaked, having splashed and dropped their way through rapid after rapid. As they moved into a calmer stretch, they were tired but exhilarated.

"Well done, you two! You looked like a proper team there, you did!"

Tori stuck her tongue out at Hudson, who returned the insult. "Oh, I don't know about that," she laughed, "more like just not wanting to get ourselves killed."

Malcolm laughed, "Well, whatever the reason, you two did well. What do you say, Seamus? Do you think we have more rapids coming, or can we have a break?"

"I think we can have a quick spot of tea up ahead," Seamus replied, "and maybe a dry off." They pulled off onto a bit of sandy beach to dry their clothes and have some light refreshment.

But truthfully, they were all anxious to get home. After a short rest and a stretch of their tired arms, they loaded back into the boat and the fast-moving water. Hours went by like minutes as the four swiftly traveled south along the raging river.

Hudson's shoulders were sore from the rowing, and his hands started to blister.

"I hope we don't have too many more rapids," he finally said. "I don't know if I can row anymore."

Seamus replied, "You've done well, Master Hudson. We're just about to pull off the North Passage and back onto the river that leads to your home. Well done. Truly. You have both done an incredible job. Absolutely top notch. I think we've set a new record for the fastest time on this stretch of river, and I couldn't have done it without your help."

Tori and Hudson smiled wearily and put the oars back into the boat.

Seamus steered them through a few more bends and then, to the right, he pulled off into a new tunnel.

"Here we are. The final stretch!"

Tori yawned loudly, "Thank goodness! I'm exhausted!"

Hudson chimed in. "Me too. I can barely sit up."

"It's okay if you take a little nap, Hudson," Malcolm replied. "We shouldn't need your steering anymore."

"Nah," he said sleepily. "I can never nap."

Instead, he looked at the walls of the caves and the glowing crystal lights, tired but awake.

After another hour on the slower river, Seamus steered left, taking them into another tunnel. Hudson could barely keep his eyes open, and Tori had dozed off once or twice. Her head would nod down onto her chest and then fling back up.

Malcolm looked back at Seamus, "They have been through quite an adventure, haven't they?"

Seamus replied warmly, "Ay, that they have. Let's get the wee ones home to their parents."

Seamus pulled off onto a sandy beach at the side of the river. As the boat eased onto the shore, they could see the opening of the hole they'd come down days before.

"That hole felt like a lifetime ago," Tori said as she got out of the boat and turned to help Hudson. "I wonder if Mom and Dad are home?" She looked at the hole, anxious to get back to their house.

"I'd imagine so," Malcolm replied, looking at a pocket watch he had in his coat. "It's quite late now."

They went to the hole in the wall that went back up to the surface. Inside the hole was a golden string. "Now, Hudson, you've not used one of these before, so let me show you," Malcolm explained. "You just take hold of the string and then put your feet here." He stepped into the hole, putting his feet at the base. Then, grabbing the gold string, he immediately started getting pulled up the hole. "And off you go!" he called back to him, disappearing from view.

Tori went next, then Hudson, then Seamus. They all put their hands on the golden string, and it swiftly pulled them up the hole to the surface like a conveyor belt.

They emerged at the base of the old walnut tree. It was dark out, and the sky was cloudy. The air was warm and humid, summertime at the farm. The crickets were singing loudly, and they heard an owl hoot in the darkness. They looked in the direction of their house.

They could see a light on in the living room. Their parents must still be up, waiting for them. Brushing the dirt from their clothes, they walked back to their house.

They were home.

Sixteen

A New Day

Tori and Hudson quietly walked up to the house, trying to surprise their parents by not alerting the dogs. They could see them sitting on the sofa, reading books by the light of a lamp, the dogs curled up next to them. They crept to the door, silently opening it.

"Hello!" Hudson called out, and their parents jumped up.

"Hudson! Tori!" they both exclaimed together. "You're home!" They rushed into a huge hug, and the dogs jumped up and down excitedly.

After hugging her parents, Tori knelt down to each dog as they licked her face. "Wow, it feels so good to be back!" The dogs wagged their tails in unison, agreeing they were happy to have their family home.

Malcolm and Seamus stood to the side, happily watching the reunion. Tori's parents turned to look at them and also gave them a huge hug. "Thank you for bringing our babies back safely. We've been so worried, but hoped everything would be okay."

"So, how did it go?" their mom asked.

Tori and Hudson started to rush out their stories. Talking over each other, they told their parents about rapids, the North Pole, elves, and crystal caves. "And there was this one cool elf named Merlin and another named Clyde who played the best music," Tori explained.

Hudson added, "And don't forget about the rapids and the super creepy forest!" Their parents wanted to ask more questions, but could tell the kids were tired, as it was almost midnight.

"Well, Hudson," their dad said, "Maybe we can hear about the creepy forest tomorrow, after you two have had a proper night's sleep in your beds. We've got the big fan set up, and the windows are open. The air conditioning doesn't work on the generator."

"Oh yeah," Tori said, remembering that when they left, the power and all the internet had been out. "Is there still no electricity?"

Their mom sighed, giving them a big hug. "No, I'm afraid not, but don't worry, we are finding ways forward. We will tell you all about it in the morning. For now, go change into your pajamas and get a good night's sleep. We are so glad to see you home." She turned to Malcolm and Seamus. "You'll stay too, right? You must be tired. We can get you set up in the guest bedroom."

"Thank you kindly, madam," Seamus said, the picture of politeness. "We're all a bit tired after the journey, aren't we?"

Hudson yawned loudly in response. The kids went up to bed, the dogs following close behind, wanting to join their favorite people.

The sun had long been up by the time the gnomes and children woke.

Malcolm, who was the early riser, even slept in past nine. The journey along the river had taken its toll, as had all the adventures of the past week. Tori's mom had a full pancake breakfast ready for them when they got up. Pancakes with chocolate chips, strawberries, blueberries, maple syrup, and whipped cream. She'd also cooked up a huge plate of bacon and eggs and a pot of tea for the gnomes.

Malcolm's eyes widened as he went into the kitchen.

"Hurry up, kids!" he called up the stairs, "Or there'll be none left for you when you get down!"

He held himself back, though, and contented himself with a cup of tea while he waited for the others. Tori's mom joined him, though she added a few ice cubes to the tea. "It's too hot outside to be drinking hot tea," she explained.

She had the windows open, and the hazy summer air brought in the sound of locusts and birds chirping.

Malcolm asked her while they waited, "How are things going here? Has there been any help from the government? Are any of the roads open? How are the people doing?"

She shook her head, "No, the government was worse than useless. Though I guess they have their own homes and families to worry about. But it's fine. Who wants a bunch of military types bossing people around, telling us what we already know how to do? Nah, we just organized as a community. We've got everything we need right here; we just hadn't realized it. Our neighbors down the way had a wood shop in their garage, and they've been helping people fix up their homes. The other neighbor's a nurse, so she's been helping anyone who was hurt. It is amazing! We had no idea we had so many talented people in our community."

Malcolm smiled, appreciating the idea of pulling together, "That's amazing. And what about the power or the internet? Have they come on at all?"

"No," she sighed. "From what we can tell, the earthquakes caused so much damage to the grid it could be years before they build it up again. But we found we are getting along okay without it all. We have our generator, and just use it at night for lights, and to keep the fridge and freezer cold. And the gas stations seem to have enough fuel since people aren't driving much with the roads all being damaged. I don't know what we are going to do long term, but we're okay for now. We've heard of a group that is trying to get solar panels out to people. But really, it's been about people connecting through word of mouth and the radio. We created a central board in town where people can post things they are offering or things they need. It seems to be working pretty well."

"That's pretty much how we gnomes live," he told her. "We have a little community center where we come together and share what we have with each other. We don't use money to buy stuff the way you do."

"Well, we don't either!" she laughed, "Not anymore. Everything was digital, even our money. You turn the power off for a week and realize pretty quickly that money is meaningless. You realize the things that matter. Your family, your home, your health, and your happiness." She paused, looking out the window and listening to the birds. "Everything else kind of falls away."

He nodded, looking at the blue sky and the trees outside.

An eruption of sound came from the stairs as the kids and dogs came clamoring into the kitchen.

"Malcolm!" Hudson cried out, "You didn't really eat all the breakfast, did you?"

Seamus walked in as well and said, "No, he didn't, but I'm about to! I'm starving! And pancakes? What a wonderful American treat!"

"You don't have pancakes where you live?" Tori asked.

"Not as delicious and fluffy as these are. They look amazing, Mrs. Johnson. Thank you." Seamus climbed up into a chair at the table and started piling his plate as high as his hat.

"Hey!" Tori cried out, "Save some for us!" They all dug into breakfast, and their mom sat back, filled with joy to have her children home again.

After they finished eating, Hudson asked his mom a strange question "Mom, did you feel a shift in the air yesterday?"

"What do you mean, Hudson?" She asked. "What kind of a shift?"

Hudson continued to be mysterious. "Oh, I don't know. Like, did something change? This Weaver elf said we changed the storyline and reset the system, but I don't know if you felt something. Like did a bell ring, or the wind blow, or something?"

His mom thought for a while, understanding his question.

"Yes, Hudson, I think we did," she replied. "We were sitting outside with the dogs, filling water from the spring, and cleaning up the garden. And your dad suddenly looked at me and he said, 'I think I'm happy for the first time in a long time.' And I looked back at him and said, 'Me too.' I mean, of course, we were still worried about you two, but something did shift. It wasn't so much in the air, it was in how we looked at things."

"Huh," he said thoughtfully, "That's pretty cool. So, I guess it worked."

She came over and hugged him. "Yes, Hudson, I don't know what the future holds. And we've still got some big problems to sort through. But I think it worked."

Their dad came in from doing barn chores and joined them at the table.

"Ooh, Dad," Tori called out, "You're so sweaty! Gross! Go take a shower!"

He laughed, "Wait until you see the solar shower we've set up outside. We're using the spring water and a mini solar panel. It's like camping every day!"

"That sounds fun," Hudson said. "I love the idea of taking a shower outside. Running around naked like a crazy person!" He laughed and gave the gnomes a wild look. They laughed too, as gnomes loved bathing in streams and rivers. They had no problems with showering in nature.

They finished breakfast, and then Malcolm and Seamus said they had to be on their way.

"So soon?" Tori asked sadly. "Can't you stay and hang out for a little while?"

"We'd love to, my dear," Malcolm said kindly, "But we need to get back to our own homes. We have to rebuild our houses and communities. We all have to create a fresh start."

Tori nodded, hugging them both tightly. "Of course, I understand, though you'll keep writing in the book, right? Who knows when we will have internet again? You're my lifeline!"

"Of course, my dear," Malcolm said, tapping his coat pocket. "I always keep that book with me, wherever I go."

"Oh, and speaking of!" he reached into his coat pocket and pulled out two envelopes. "These are the letters from Merlin for each of you! How could I have almost forgotten them?"

He handed one to each child. Their names were written on the front in a beautiful flowing scroll. The ink was gold and shimmered on the page, moving slightly.

"Wow," their mom looked at the envelopes. "Those look fancy. Let's put them here on the counter so you can read them after you've said goodbye to your friends."

The family walked outside with Malcolm and Seamus, taking them back to the walnut tree.

Hudson was sad as he hugged the gnomes. "I'm going to miss you both. We had such a great time. When will I see you again?"

Seamus gave Hudson a long hug, "I don't know when, but I know that friends like us always bump back into each other again. Until then, keep out of trouble, lad. Or at least if you keep into trouble, let it be all the fun sorts."

He winked and then turned around to face the whole family. He bowed his head slightly and said, "It's never goodbye, but until next time."

Then he and Malcolm turned to look at each other. Malcolm smiled,

"Shall we?"

Seamus grinned, "Absolutely!"

They gave both kids a wink and then, together, jumped down into the hole at the base of the walnut tree. And just like that, they were gone.

Tori sighed, and Hudson frowned. Their dad put his arms around both of them and slowly walked with them back to the house.

Back inside, Tori remembered the letters from Merlin. She handed one to Hudson and opened hers. They each had the same letter inside, written with beautiful gold ink. This is what the letter said.

Dear Children,

Each of us is a color of thread.

We all have our gifts to bring. What do we do in this time of so many endings? We bring our gifts. Some of us are red, some are yellow, some are brown, and some are blue. Some are Weavers of stories, some are builders, and some are healers. Some manage, some work in the background, some dream, and some do. Some are great at school, and some want to live in the woods, talking to the trees. But each of us is here for a reason, and the biggest reason is to learn who we really are. To learn that our gifts are perfect, even if others may call them different or strange. We Weavers understand this. That is why the tapestry is full of every color of the rainbow. And don't let anyone else tell you differently.

This is how we build the world anew. This is how we dream ourselves out of the old nightmare. We build bridges of colors and buildings of light. We connect, thread to thread, to make the most beautiful tapestry imaginable. And here we shall see that we are all connected in the great story of life.

Fate is not our enemy but the framework to help us shine. The mists you traveled through to find us were not there just to slow you down but to help you grow. And the challenges you went through to get to where you are right now are what will make you shine.

So choose your thread, and know that whatever you choose, it is always the right choice. Follow your heart, and don't let go of your dreams for a brighter world. They will always show you the way.

With Love,

Merlin

Epilogue

Six months after what had been called The Great Reset, life for Tori and Hudson had settled into a new rhythm. School had started again, but it was very different than before. They spent time each day in the forest, learning about the different plants that grew there. They learned what was safe to eat, what could heal cuts, and what to avoid.

Learning about gardening and forestry was now as much a part of their day as math and writing. This was both practical and fun. Stores didn't carry a huge range of medicines like they used to. Stores didn't carry much at all, since transportation and manufacturing had ground to a halt.

They still didn't have reliable internet or cell service. They could get messages to other cities using telephone lines that some creative engineers had pieced together. Their mom had spent a month trying to track down all their family members. She'd been able to confirm their grandparents and two aunts were safe, but she'd never been able to find another aunt and two cousins. They kept hope, but realized many people had been lost in the earthquakes, tornadoes, and floods. Life for Tori and Hudson was finding the balance between that sadness and the hope they'd discovered with the Weavers.

A few areas had gotten electricity restored, but not near their farm. The gas stations had finally run out of fuel, and so did the generator and the tractor. They were learning to live without electricity, cooking and cleaning the way people did 100 years ago. Hudson thought it was great fun, but it was a hard adjustment for their Mom and Dad. Life on a farm without electricity was hard work! Days were very busy, and nights were very quiet.

The government was slowly coming back to life. Not quite like it was before. It was a softer, gentler, and more helpful government. It cared about the well-being of the people. Money had disappeared when the internet did. It didn't matter how much money someone had in a bank if they couldn't access it with a credit card or cell phone. So, people started doing things just to help each other, not make money. A program had been rolled out to get a solar panel to each house, so people had enough electricity to run a light or two at night, a fan in the summer, and a heater in the winter.

They used to spend all their days riding in the car, going to school, hockey practice, ice skating competitions, and shopping. Now their days were a lot simpler. Hudson missed hockey, but he found new adventures in the woods around his house. He even discovered a family of gnomes that lived not far from the farm. And his hockey team was arranging some hockey games on the local pond, now that it was winter.

Tori had found new paths in the woods and rode to her friend's house with her mountain bike. She'd take their horse sometimes, but usually her parents rode the horses to the community center. The community center had become the life of the town. People would gather, trade, and share.

At first, there was so much sadness as people realized the extent of the devastation. But through the recovery, people came together closer than ever. They felt grateful for what they had and were willing to help out their neighbors. There were still disagreements. People hadn't changed completely, but everything felt a bit softer and slower. And the most unusual thing of all was that the adults started to look to the children for guidance.

The children had great ideas on how to set up things in a new way. They could see how to bring people together or create new ways of sharing supplies. They had a certain creativity that the adults lacked. There were many nights when Hudson would share an idea or two that his dad then took to the community center the next day. And it wasn't just Hudson.

Tori helped create a group of girls and boys who'd visit the seniors. With no internet, many people had lost their links to family and friends. Tori's group helped fill the gap by visiting older people who didn't have family nearby. They ended up receiving as much love and kindness, if not more, than they were giving.

Life had its challenges as the world rebuilt. But it was a new way of being, one filled with sunsets and conversations, instead of to-do lists and social media. It was filled with kindness to strangers and generosity to neighbors. Tori kept in touch with Malcolm and Seamus. They were also rebuilding their lives, though the gnomes already lived without electricity and cell phones. But they told her that the humans around the world were all coming out of this softer and gentler. They were happy to see it, though it had been hard in the making.

Tori wondered if people would fall back to their old ways when the power was restored. She liked this new way of living. She could feel all the things the children had put into the Tapestry up at the North Pole. A better government, a fluffier and softer way of being, no murders or crimes, and people supporting each other during hard times. If she had anything to say about it, she'd keep it this way.

The North Passage

About the Author

Erin Lucero is an author, architect, and nature lover from Colorado. Whether it's writing or designing, she loves turning dreams into realities. Her books all share a common theme – the importance of finding our inner light, embracing adventure, and rediscovering the magic in the world.

Erin believes in the power of storytelling as a way of turning complex ideas into magical adventures. Her writing voice has been called warm and approachable, like talking to an old friend. She published the non-fiction book Ayni as a personal journey and a road map to finding self-love and harmony through the teachings of yoga and shamanism. She has also published a children's book called Hudson and the Magic Crow, which teaches children how big an impact humans can have in the world, and how what we do matters. She cares deeply for Mother Earth and all her children and making this planet a better place for all living things.

Erin graduated with honors from Rensselaer Polytechnic Institute with a Bachelor of Architecture and a minor in communications and has had a lifelong love of writing and creative expression. She began writing poems and short essays at a young age, winning local awards and publishing her work in local newspapers. She took pen back to paper to tell stories she wished she had been able to tell her young self. Her book Quest for the Phoenix, a Book Life Review Editors' pick, tells the story of a 10-year-old girl choosing love and support over fear as she joins two gnomes on an adventure of a lifetime to save a dying phoenix. The North Passage continues the story of Tori and the gnomes, finding inspiration and hope in a world full of challenges.

You can connect with me on:
🌐 http://erinlucero.com

Subscribe to my newsletter:
✉ https://erinlucero.com/contact

Also by Erin Lucero

Erin writes stories about finding our inner light, embracing adventure, and rediscovering the magic in the world.

Quest for the Phoenix

When Tori saw what she thought was a garden gnome in her backyard, little did she guess the adventures that would await her. Armed with kindness, compassion, and a few funny jokes, this young girl sets out on the quest of a lifetime – to help the magical phoenix be reborn, and prevent the world from falling into darkness. She travels underground rivers, meets magical creatures, and overcomes great obstacles in her quest for the phoenix. Along the way, Tori will also discover just how much magic she has inside herself, and if a single young girl can save the entire world.

Hudson and the Magic Crow

Hudson is a kind and thoughtful little boy who lives on a farm with his horse, goats, chickens, and lots of dogs. One special day he meets a magical crow who shows him how to fly.

Together, they see the world through the eyes of the crow and learn just how big an impact humans have on the world around them. Hudson learns how he can help the crow and all the plants and animals in nature, and make it a happier place for all the living things.

Ayni: Finding Connection, Love & Harmony with the Wisdom of Yoga and Shamanism

Ayni, a word from the Andes, is a concept that all things are connected. If we live in generosity and abundance, the universe will reciprocate that abundance. It's a way of life that teaches balance with the Earth and love for all living things. Join Erin Lucero as she weaves together the teachings of Tantric Yoga and Peruvian Shamanism to find that love, balance, and harmony in our own lives, and to rekindle that connection with the World.

The Wisdom of Hummingbird

Discover the wisdom of the Royal Hummingbird, a symbol of radiance and love across many cultures. Author and healer Erin Lucero shares the teachings she received contemplating this powerful archetype. She explores the lessons of seeing things as they are, the power of stillness, unconditional love, and stepping into courageous creation.

www.ingramcontent.com/pod-product-compliance
Lightning Source LLC
Chambersburg PA
CBHW020637110726
47899CB00002B/809